The Queen of Speckled Wood

Written and illustrated by
S.W. TEAL

Text and illustrations copyright © S.W. Teal 2017

S.W. Teal asserts the moral right to be identified as the author and illustrator of this work.

ISBN-10: 1542958741
ISBN-13: 978-1542958745

All rights reserved. No part of this publication may be reproduced, stored in a retrieval system, or transmitted in any form or by any means without the prior consent of the publishers.

This book is sold subject to the condition that it shall not, by way of trade or otherwise, be lent, re-sold, hired out, or otherwise circulated without the publisher's prior consent in any form of binding or cover other than that in which it is published.

- CHAPTER 1 -

The ancient oak tree stood majestic, surrounded by its own kind. A deep, cavernous hollow in its mighty trunk served as the perfect hideout. Maela could smell the air outside; thick, damp, full of change. When the wind wasn't chasing the leaves off the trees, she could hear the trickle of the nearby stream. It somehow soothed her uneasiness of living alone. She would often sit at the water's edge and make a wish in the hope that it would be granted further downstream, but two cycles of the moon had passed and still her family had not returned.

From within the hollow, Maela looked out into the darkness. Falling leaves came to rest on the woodland floor as the wind ceased its playful game. The far-off tunes of a blackbird could then be heard, echoing through the air. Maela often dreamed of following his enticing song, wanting to believe that he was calling her to a more welcoming, less hostile part of the woodland. But she could not leave. How could she? She still clung onto the hope that one day her family would return and that life would be full of excitement and adventure once more. How she dreamed of playing hide and seek with her two brothers again, and hearing the sweet voice of her mother calling her home at meal times.

The moon edged into view, full and bright, and Maela welcomed its presence with a faint smile. She then shuffled back, deeper into the hollow that was now her home, and there she began to sing a song that her mother had once taught her, enjoying the acoustic vibrations around her.

If only the trees could talk
I'd have much to say
About the way
I feel so alone on their canopy-moulting bay.

Mother Beech would take me aside
In her thick dark branches I would hide.
And she would describe –

Snap!

In a heartbeat, Maela stopped singing and stared, wide-eyed, out into the woodland, the words of the song temporarily forgotten. Silver patches of moonlight flickered in the breeze, but nothing else caught her eye. 'An acorn,' she told herself. 'It was just an acorn falling from the tree.' After convincing herself that all was well, she took a few deep breaths before continuing with her song.

And she would describe her hundred years past
How her sisters fell when men came fast.

If only the trees could talk
I'd fill my day
In the –

Snap!

Another acorn? This time Maela was not so sure. Careful not to make a sound, she shuffled as far back into the hollow as she could. Her senses were alive. Raising her snout, she caught a distinct musty smell in the air. Her heart thumped against her chest as she wondered what to do.

'Do not stop,' came a soft voice from somewhere close by. 'Please, continue your song. For I have passed by here many a time just to hear your sweet voice – your sweet, enchanting voice.'

From within the tree, Maela shuddered, making her hair stand firm on end.

'I mean you no harm,' the soft voice went on. 'Please, continue.'

Unable to see who the voice was coming from, Maela felt impelled to speak. 'If you mean me no harm,' she trembled, 'then why do you not show yourself?'

After a brief pause, the soft voice spoke again, closer this time. 'Forgive me,' it said, and a moment later a shiny black nose came into Maela's view. A long snout followed; russet red and perfectly formed.

Soon there stood before her the most handsome creature that Maela had ever seen. 'You ... you are a fox!' she exclaimed.

'Indeed I am,' the fox replied.

'But ...' Maela hesitated, 'I have heard much about your kind, and I do not think that you are to be trusted.'

'I do not know what you have heard about my kind, but let me assure you once more, I mean you no harm.' The fox lowered himself down onto the fallen leaves and narrowed his eyes, peering into the dark hollow of the oak tree. Two tiny specks of light stared back at him. 'Now that you have seen me, is it not fair that I should now see you?'

Again Maela shuddered. She wanted to trust the fox, believing that there was something familiar about his voice. But how could she when she brought to mind everything that she had ever heard about his kind? 'Before I allow you to see me,' she whispered, 'will you do me one thing? Will you close your eyes and let your senses guide your instincts?'

'I will do as you ask.' Without delay, the fox closed his eyes and raised his snout so that it pointed directly at the tree.

Maela edged forward until the light of the moon rested upon the tip of her soft, black nose. 'Can you not smell me?' she asked. 'Can you not smell what I am? Does my scent not fill you with aggression?'

'Aggression?' the fox exclaimed. 'No! Enchantment? Yes. Curiosity? Maybe, for now I think I know what you are, and if I am right, then I stand firm by my word. You have nothing to fear from me.'

'Then I will take you at your word.' Keeping a cautious eye on the fox, Maela crept out of the hollow. 'You now may open your eyes.'

Lowering his snout, the fox was not altogether surprised by what now stood before him. He tilted his head to one side, mesmerised by the female's black and white facial stripes.

'Why do you stare so?' the young badger asked. 'You claimed you knew what I was, yet you continue to fathom me.'

'Forgive me,' the fox diverted his gaze, 'for it is your beauty that captivates me.'

When their eyes met again, Maela noticed a change in the fox's expression, almost as though he recognised her.

'Will you sing to me again?' he asked. 'Will you fill my ears with the sweetest of melodies that I yearn to hear every moment of every day?'

It had been so long since Maela had had anyone to talk to, let alone to sing to, so she raised herself up in preparation. The fox settled himself down, curled his thick brush tail about him, and closed his eyes.

If only the trees could talk
I'd fill my day
In the daylight ray
Listening to tales of the old wood way.

Father Oak would whisper in my ear
Of how the trees as gods strike immortal animal fear.
And how he had chosen me
As his new variety of animal tree.

If only the trees could talk
I would pray
On every day
For a special someone to come my way.

- CHAPTER 2 -

The moon drifted soundlessly across the night sky. Clouds shifted, and a subtle breeze cooled the woodland air.

When the fox awoke from a dreamless sleep, he found that he was alone. Raising his head, he scoured the darkness, desperate to seek out his new companion, but there was no sign of her. His eyes then rested upon the oak tree and he sniffed at the air. He got to his feet and approached the hollow entrance with caution.

'Are you there?' he whispered. The badger's scent was rife, but there was no reply. The fox extended his neck, allowing his snout to enter the hollow and, with added curiosity, he began to paw at the ground.

'You will find nothing there,' came an agitated voice behind him.

Caught off guard, the fox made to retreat, but hit his head sharply against the top of the entrance.

'Serves you right!'

Slightly abashed, the fox turned to find the outline of his new companion sitting high upon a leaf-covered mound, her white stripes glinting silver in the fading moonlight. 'Forgive me,' he said. 'I did not see you there. Where is it that you have been?'

'Foraging,' Maela replied.

'Why then did you not wake me? I should have liked to have come with you.' The thought of food was now prevalent in the fox's mind.

Maela hesitated. 'From what I have heard about your kind, if I had woken you from your sleep you may have attacked me.'

'I do not know from where you have heard these tales about my kind, but let me assure you of one thing at least: I would never harm you. To harm you would be like bringing harm upon myself. You are already dear to me, young badger, but I fear you do not yet hold trust in me. What must I do further to gain your trust?'

'Tell me your name.'

'I am Firana,' the fox announced, 'but you can call me Fira – most of my kind do.'

'I am not of your kind, but Fira I will call you. It is a name not common to me, but it fits you well.'

'What then am I to call you?' Fira asked.

'I am Maela.'

'Maela?' Fira looked long at his new companion for he knew that name well. At length he began to edge closer to where she sat, his mind filling with endless possibilities. 'But surely you are not ... No, you cannot be. You are far too young.'

'What is this that you speak of?' Maela asked. 'What am I too young for? And why do you stare at me so?'

Fira had not meant to speak his last thoughts aloud,

but he could no longer keep from Maela what he knew. 'Forgive me,' he began, 'but Maela is the name of our queen. I am trying to find her. I merely thought that –'

'That I was Queen?' Maela laughed. But her expression soon faltered. 'Am I then to understand that the queen is not known to you?'

'Quite the opposite,' Fira replied. 'In fact I know her well, or at least I thought I did. But she has not been seen or heard of for some time now and there are rumours spreading that she may no longer be in this world.'

'I see.' This news deeply troubled Maela and she began to scratch needlessly at the fallen leaves before her.

'But this need not worry you,' Fira continued, noting her reaction. 'I am sure that your mother merely named you after the Queen of Speckled Wood because you reflect the characteristic of her beauty.'

Maela looked up. 'Then was the queen a badger, like me?' she asked.

'Why, yes. Some say that she was the finest looking creature in this land, and I would have to agree. It troubles me so that she was taken from us so suddenly.'

'She was taken?'

'Well, I say taken, only because of the rumours. We have held many searches throughout this woodland, but all traces of her have since gone. It is said that she was last seen in this region and I was appointed the task of searching here. Many times I have passed through here and that is how I came to hear your beautiful singing.'

'Who appointed you?'

'The Chief of the Council. Regularly we meet to discuss the needs of the woodland. It is a bitter time at present – with no ruler and no guide – and many fear that man's destruction will fall upon us all too soon as it did to the neighbouring woodland not so long ago.'

'But what can be done?' asked Maela, troubled at hearing such news. 'Surely we cannot fight against the power of man. It would be folly to even try such a thing.'

'There are ways,' Fira said, 'but I am not at liberty to disclose them to you out of Council. But rest assured, dear Maela, we are doing all that we can.'

Again, Maela scratched at the leaves before her. 'Are there any more of my kind at your Council?' she asked.

'Why, yes,' Fira replied. 'I have already spoken of him. He is named Balorn, Chief of the Council.'

With increased interest, Maela fixed her eyes upon Fira's. 'Then I should very much like to meet him.'

'And meet him you shall. But not this night.' Fira looked overhead and noticed that the moon had long since passed from view. 'It is late,' he went on, 'and I must now return to the others. They will be waiting on my report. Farewell, dear Maela.'

As Fira turned to leave, Maela called his name. 'I do trust you, though right now I cannot prove it.' She lowered her head and began to root her nose amongst the leaves. She then stepped forward, stopping as close as she dare in front of Fira, and dropped something at his feet. 'In accepting this gift that I bring to you, it will be a mark that you promise to honour my trust.'

Fira looked down and saw before him a string of alder cones. 'I accept your gift,' he said. 'But you do not have to prove your trust in me.' He took the cones between his teeth and gave Maela one last, woeful look, before disappearing into the night.

- CHAPTER 3 -

The weak, autumn sun crept into the sky, casting a dappled light to spread across the woodland floor. As the light grew stronger, filtering through the mist, it revealed an array of earthly colours, and the distant, unwavering song of the blackbird could be heard once more.

Maela could not sleep. Several times she got up and rearranged her bedding, but in doing so she caught the scent of Fira and was reminded of their conversation. The words that he had spoken to her played upon her mind. Hearing about the Queen of the Speckled Wood was news to her and she was eager to learn more.

After finally drifting into an uneasy sleep, she felt as though she was searching for something – something that she had not seen for a very long time. She was digging deep into the ground, turning over heavy rocks, but time was running out and she needed to find it. Someone else was looking for it also; someone whom she knew would not appreciate it and would use it only for their good. Where was it? What was it? Why was it now down to her to find it?

She turned rigidly in her sleep, as though preparing to fight. 'It is mine!' she exclaimed. 'It is mine! You have no right to touch it!' She kicked frantically at her bedding and struggled to stand. 'I will not let you have it! It is mine!'

The woodland was in darkness when Maela woke with a start. There were voices just outside. One of them she recognised as Fira's, but the other was not known to her. Ignoring the pounding of her heart, she edged forward, desperate to catch what was being said. At the entrance of the hollow, she allowed her nose to touch the cool evening air, when a familiar scent – much stronger than that of Fira's – filled her senses with desire. Her curiosity was now so intense that she bravely stepped out of the tree. At once she laid eyes upon the familiar, welcoming form of Fira. Standing beside him was another of her kind.

'Hullo,' Fira bowed. 'I hope we did not disturb you.'

Staring deep into the eyes of the powerful, young badger, Maela was at a loss for words. She simply shook her head in response.

'Maela, this is Balorn, Chief of the Council,' Fira announced. 'And Balorn, this is Maela.'

Balorn bowed graciously at hearing her name. 'Very pleased I am to meet you,' he said in a voice that held much authority. 'Tell me, Maela, how long have you lived here alone?'

'Two moons,' Maela replied timidly.

'It grieves me to hear that, for I did not realise that anyone still dwelt this far west. The first I heard of you was from Fira here, last night. Had I known sooner, then you should not have had to live in such seclusion for so long.'

'It matters not,' Maela shrugged, still captivated by Balorn's presence. 'I have had my memories for company.'

'Well, you need be alone no longer,' Balorn stood proud. 'My family dwells in the east and we would welcome you to stay with us.'

'You are too kind,' Maela shied away, 'but I cannot leave.' She gazed upon her oak tree with sadness in her eyes. 'It may not look much to you, but to me, this is my home.'

'I do not wish to part you from your home, Maela. I merely wish to set my mind at ease and see that you are safe.'

'Safe from what?' Maela enquired. 'No one has passed through here these last two moons, save Fira. I cannot think of a safer place to be.'

'It is man that we fear,' Fira explained, dropping his voice to almost a whisper. 'I already mentioned to you the threat of destruction, but it now seems that we have underestimated man's power and speed. Last night, one of our council members – a grey squirrel, named Sirus – came back with news that men have already been sighted not far from here.'

'But what do they want?'

'Simply to claim this land for their own use. If what Sirus tells us is true, then they mean to destroy this part of the woodland and everything that lives here. But what then is to stop them encroaching further and destroying the whole of Speckled Wood?'

'We must act fast,' Balorn warned, 'before this goes too far. I fear we may not have more than a few nights before the devastation begins.'

Maela shook her head in disbelief.

'I know that this is hard for you,' Balorn said, 'but you need to trust in what I tell you. It is not safe for you to remain here alone.'

'No,' Maela dismissed his warning. 'I cannot leave. I need to be here. Please understand. I need to be here when my family return. They need to see that I am –' she caught sight of Balorn's woeful look. She had no need to say any more.

Balorn bowed graciously, then announced that it was time for him to depart. 'Think about what I have said,' he told Maela finally, 'and I will see you again very soon.' He bowed once more, then turned away, leaving Fira and Maela alone.

'I understand that you do not wish to leave here,' Fira said, 'so would you at least allow me to stay with you and see that you are safe from harm?'

'You also are too kind,' Maela replied, 'but I would not have you burden yourself for me.'

'It would be no burden, I assure you. To see you safe is all that I desire.'

Taking only a moment to consider this, Maela decided to accept his offer. 'You may stay here this night,' she told him, 'but that is all. Once the dawn arrives you must return to your home.'

'But the light of day is to be feared far more than the night,' Fira protested. 'Will you not reconsider?'

Seeming to ignore his words, Maela turned and began to head south. 'Walk with me,' she said.

Fira hurried to her side. 'Where are we going?'

'To the stream. There is something that I want you to see.'

As they walked, Maela became aware of a strange rustling noise, different to that of the leaves, and soon realised that it was coming from Fira. She glanced down and saw that he had something attached to one his forelegs. It was the string of alder cones that she had presented to him the night before. He had skilfully formed it into a ring and had secured it just above his right paw.

'Do you not eat the fruits of the alder?' she enquired.

Her words prompted Fira to look down at his leg. 'Occasionally I do,' he told her. 'However, it seemed more fitting that, as it was a gift, I should keep hold of it. I wear it as a mark of honour.'

The sound of babbling water was all around them and Maela stopped just short of the narrow stream's edge. She sat down and peered through the darkness to the other side, deliberately avoiding Fira's gaze. 'Why do you honour me so?' she asked. 'What have I done to deserve such recognition?'

'You have given me your trust,' Fira replied. 'That is all.'

'So, it is not to do with my name?'

Fira joined Maela in looking to the other side of the stream. 'It is true,' he began, 'that at first, I felt it my duty to protect you because of your name. But your trust in me is worth far more than any title, especially in the light of what you have heard about my kind.'

'Then may I ask you this once to prove your honour?' Maela spoke openly. 'For I now need to trust you to look away. There is something that I must collect, but I do not yet feel ready to disclose its location.'

Slightly cautious of her meaningless words, Fira did as she asked without question.

'I will not be gone long,' Maela told him. She then set off upstream.

Respectfully, Fira kept his eyes fixed due east. Every now and then he heard a rustling behind him in the distance and he hoped with all his heart that the sound was coming from Maela. She had left him in a perilous position.

Maela moved with stealth, keeping her footing to the rocks beside the stream. She changed direction frequently in case Fira was trying to keep track of her. True to her word, she was not gone long, and on her return she moved back on to the fallen leaves to make her presence known. She was carrying something in her mouth, which she placed carefully on the ground before her.

'You may now turn around,' she announced, 'but be careful of where you place your paws.'

Fira began to twist his neck around as far as he could to see what it was that he should avoid treading on. At first he could see nothing but leaves on the ground, but on closer inspection ...

His jaw dropped. For a moment he seemed to have forgotten that the rest of his body was still facing the other way, but gradually he began to untwist himself, not daring to peel his eyes away from the thing that Maela had presented him with. 'Is that –?' he uttered uneasily. 'Is that what I think it is?'

Uncertain that she had done the right thing, Maela simply nodded, and said, 'Yes. I believe that is what you have been searching for.'

- CHAPTER 4 -

Some time passed before Fira felt able to start questioning Maela as to the nature of her business there. 'So, you do know of the Queen of Speckled Wood,' he said, slight desperation in his voice. 'Have I until now been wasting my time?'

'No,' Maela replied. 'For I have not deceived you.'

'Then how did you know about this?' Fira pawed at the ground before him, not daring to touch the delicate structure that lay there. 'Only one who is close to the queen would surely know of this.'

'I cannot tell you what you want to hear, Fira.'

'Cannot or will not?'

'Please, do not ask me any more, for you have a look in your eye that I could tell you all that your heart desires to hear.' Maela lowered her gaze and stared mournfully at the structure.

'I know not what to make of this,' Fira sighed with discontent, 'but I must report it. Balorn of the Council needs to be informed. This changes everything. It could lead us to answering all of our questions. At the very least it is a sign of hope that good tidings are abound!'

'Do what you will, but do not involve me. I have done my part and I cannot give you any more.' Maela stooped to retrieve the structure, then began to walk away.

'Where are you going?' Fira called after her. 'You cannot take that!'

Maela did not reply, but continued back towards her hollow. She heard Fira coming up behind her and so she picked up her pace, but she could not outrun the fox.

'Stop!' Fira overtook Maela and barred her way, looming over her with terrifying intent.

Unwavering, Maela set the structure down. 'What right do you have to order me?'

'You cannot take that,' Fira persisted, calming his tone. 'I must return with it to the Council.'

'It is mine!' Maela exclaimed. 'And I will do with it what I will. Now please, let me pass.'

There was a hint of desperation in the badger's eyes and Fira could not abide to think that he had brought such anguish upon his new companion. He looked wilfully overhead. 'It is late into the night,' he said at last, 'and I must now return. Come with me, Maela, and bring that with you.'

But Maela's determination was not to be surpassed. 'If you must go, then go, but I am staying here. I did not ask for your guidance and I did not ask for your companionship. Leave now, and do not bother me again.'

'I also did not ask for your companionship, Maela,

and I did not ask for you to present me with the crown of our queen. But now that you have, you are very much involved in all of this. There are many things that the Council will wish to know from you, Maela. You cannot escape this. Tell me now all that you know and let us put an end to this feud.'

Maela held silent and began to scratch at the base of the crown as though she had only just learnt what it was.

'Is it so,' Fira went on, 'that maybe you do not hold trust in me after all?'

With the crown continuing to hold her attention, Maela finally found solace in her thoughts. 'I do trust you, Fira, for you have shown me no reason not to.'

'Then honour that trust and come with me. I will not rest easy if you remain here alone.'

'I cannot go with you,' Maela insisted. 'You do not understand. I am needed here.'

'By whom?'

'By my family.'

Maela's eyes began to glisten in the moonlight and Fira knew that there was no hope in trying to change the young badger's mind.

'Very well,' he sighed at last, 'I will leave you now. I can see that you hold many burdens here. But I promise you I will return. Come night or day, I will return.'

*

Safely back in her hollow, Maela struggled to piece together the events of the last two nights. The crown of leaves was in front of her and, as she continued to stare at it, she recollected some of the tales that her mother had told her about Speckled Wood. As the words filtered their way through her mind, she began to sing:

When my leaves have fallen
They must soon be found,
For her fate is bound
And upon her their beauty must then lie sound.

This woodland around me is mine.
But as night grows long
The feelings grow strong
That here in this realm we'll no longer belong.

When my leaves have fallen
I'll not see through the night.
May her future be bright,
For there has to be hope then to make the wrongs right.

Ever we dwell within man's eye.
We are put to the test
But they will not rest
Ere the day the leaves are all gone from the West.

The melody was sweet – Maela had always thought so, but back when her mother used to sing it, the words had been meaningless. Now, gradually, every word was beginning to make sense, and Maela at last realised the extent to which she was now involved in the search for the Queen of Speckled Wood.

- CHAPTER 5 -

Shards of daylight began to dapple the woodland floor, creating a mosaic of golden hues. It had been a long night. The news had spread fast about the discovery of the crown of leaves and so the distant voice of the blackbird now carried a long-awaited song of hope through the trees. If Maela had been aware of the sound she would have noticed the change, but her eyes were tightly shut and her breathing was unusually shallow. Locked in a harrowing dream of torment and cruel devastation, all she could hear was the voice of her mother calling to her. 'Run, Maela! Run! They are coming!'

Maela blindly turned this way and that. 'Where are you?' she called out. 'I cannot see you!'

'Run!' came the reply. 'Run like fire! There is nothing more that can be done for me. Save yourself, sweet Maela, and take all that you have of me with you!'

A low thud trembled the earth beneath where Maela lay. She snapped her eyes wide open and for a moment wondered how much of it had been a dream. Cautiously, she peered outside, squinting against the hazy sunlight. All was well, or so she hoped. Shuffling back inside, as far back as she could go, she quickly rearranged her bedding and settled herself back down. A quick glance at the crown of leaves beside her eased her anxiety and she closed her eyes.

Another low thud: louder this time, and undeniably closer. This was no dream.

Maela sprang to her feet, but did not need to go any nearer to the entrance to see, or smell, that something was occurring.

Trampling feet surrounded her, deep voices shouting. Another thud shook the very roots of her beloved tree. 'What is to be done?' she thought. 'They will catch me for certain!'

She crouched at the back of the hollow and buried her face in her bedding. There she cowered, fraught with terror, shivering, offering up words of desperation to her mother. 'How I wish I had listened to you sooner. You were trying to warn me, but I thought that I would be safe here.' The deep voices sent a chill through Maela's spine as though cold steel had penetrated her skin. 'Is there no hope?' she cried.

Whether she drifted into an uneasy sleep or whether her mother was actually there with her, Maela could not tell. A warm sensation spread through her, relieving her of her chill. Then a soft voice spoke. 'There is always hope, my sweet Maela. Remember that. Though you may often cast doubt upon it. They do not know that you are here, but others do. Run, now, and follow the wind! Run and do not look back!'

Maela squeezed her eyelids tight, forcing a single tear to break through. 'Is there to be no end in sight?' She could not remain there and risk being found. She had to run. She had no choice. She had to run like fire with only hope to cling to.

Summoning up all of her strength, she approached the entrance. No men were in sight, though their scent remained rife. Maela crouched back, ready to run, when the soft voice returned. 'Remember, Maela, take all that you have of me with you.'

'The crown!' Maela retrieved it at once.

'Follow the wind,' she was reminded, and with that firmly in mind she took off at speed, faster than she had ever run before, and did not dare look back.

The wind was strong and, with the hair on her back raised, it carried Maela so that she covered a great distance easily in half the time thought possible. Always she thought of her mother's voice. Had it really been her? Had she been watching over her and protecting her all this time? Whatever the answers, Maela knew that she had to continue, to get as far away as possible from the place that had long since been her home, but just where she was heading to she did not know.

There was a sense of foreboding about the tree that she had abandoned. Fast becoming the focus of attention, several pairs of eyes were now fixed upon it, staring intently at its darkened hollow. Maela's escape had not gone unnoticed.

Two men began to discuss what they had seen, unable to agree on what the young badger had been carrying in its mouth. They had never seen anything like it. A rustling in the leaves distracted their thoughts for a brief moment, before they decided that there was only one way of finding out what the object was.

At length, Maela began to tire and her pace began to ease. She had travelled far, but the wind was still urging her on as though it knew of some impending danger. Just ahead of her, Maela noticed a narrow stream. It could have been part of her own stream, she thought, and so she stopped there to catch her breath, setting the crown of leaves down. With the wind billowing behind her, she rested her paw carefully upon the crown so that it would not blow away. She then looked to the other side of the stream. 'Which way now?' she thought to herself. 'If I am to follow the wind, then surely I am to cross the stream.'

With no obvious way to cross it, Maela thought back to the words of her mother and tried hard to remember any further instruction. The wind seemed to be growing impatient and, whilst Maela was distracted, a sound like the screech of an owl split the air.

Shaking off her thoughts, Maela turned. 'All right!' she said, as though telling the wind to be quiet.

But the screech that she had heard had not come from the wind. Glancing further behind her, Maela realised to her horror that she was not alone. Two men, dressed in dark clothing, were approaching her, their branchlike arms outstretched.

The hair on Maela's back prickled with urgency. She had to move. And fast! Fearing for her life, she took off downstream, not daring to look back. Faster and faster she ran, keeping as close to the stream's edge as she could. The image of the two men was planted firmly in her mind, but she could only wonder at why they were chasing her. 'What do they want with me?' she cried as she ran.

The wind continued to urge her on, but before long Maela's pace began to ease. The way before her was becoming increasingly difficult to negotiate, with large rocks seeming to appear from nowhere. The stream was also becoming noticeably wider. 'How am I to cross it now?' she thought.

She had entered a part of the woodland that was densely packed with trees of the like that she had not seen before; their unusual forms twisting and coiling. Shadows were forming, and all around her indistinct voices were being carried on the wind. Maela looked up into the canopy, towering above her. Her world was spiralling away from her, leaving her far behind, helpless and abandoned until she could go on no more. She lost her footing and tripped over one of the rocks beside the stream. There she fell forward, her nose landing painfully in the cold, shallow water below.

- CHAPTER 6 -

The wind ruffled relentlessly through Maela's coarse hair, insisting that she continue her journey. But she could not move. Her whole body ached and her left foreleg burned with a pain far deeper that any blade of steel could cut. She had no concept of how long she had been there. 'What hope is there now?' she cried.

'There is every hope,' came a soft, familiar voice. 'But you must not delay.'

'I have failed you. Forgive me, I cannot go on.' Maela closed her eyes and allowed her head to sink lower into the water.

'You must go on,' the voice insisted. 'This is not your time. You must get up and fight this.'

Weary with pain and burdened with anguish, Maela felt something pulling on the back of her neck. Too weak to resist, she allowed herself to be lifted out of the water to the other side of the stream. 'Mother,' she called. 'I cannot do this. Do not ask me to.'

'The will of your mother is behind you, Maela, I see that now. And she has brought you this far. But do you not know who I am?'

Maela raised her head and saw before her the outline of a fox. 'Fira,' she whimpered. 'I have failed you also. If I had done as you desired –'

'Now is not the time, Maela. We must go. Danger is upon us and we cannot delay.'

'But my leg,' Maela protested. 'I cannot move it.'

'You have no choice. It will only worsen if you remain here. It is far better that you move now and go forward to safety.'

Using what little strength she had left, Maela struggled to her feet. She kept her left foreleg raised slightly and dared to look at it. It appeared more than twice its normal size. 'Are you to come with me?' she asked. 'I do not know where I am to go.'

'Continue your path,' Fira told her, 'and I will follow on when I can. But first I must see to it that the impending danger does not pass this stream. Go now, and make haste as best you can. Run, dear Maela. Follow the wind and do not look back!'

Having heard these words before, Maela stared uncertainly at Fira, but was soon on her way again, galloping arduously with only the wind as her guide. Sustaining her pace with apparent ease and dodging every large rock that she came to, she knew at last where it was that the wind was leading her. Her hope was kept alive now by an unmistakeable scent. She was heading straight for Balorn's sett.

Not daring to look back, she hoped with all her heart that Fira was not far behind. She could still remember every harsh word that she had spoken to him the night before and wished that she had listened to him and not been so stubborn.

Weaving her way through the trees, Maela at last saw a clearing before her. She slowed down on her approach and looked around, hoping to find something to eat there. Stopping close the centre, she fought to catch her breath and immediately felt the pain in her foreleg worsen. She wondered how much further she would have to run, and indeed whether running was still necessary. In the relative calm of the clearing it seemed as though the danger had passed and she hoped that Fira would soon catch up with her. The wind had at last died down, as though it too was taking the opportunity to rest, but then, without warning, it gathered in strength again, whirling around the clearing, telling Maela that her journey was not yet over. Instinctively, Maela outstretched a paw to stop the crown of leaves from blowing away, but as she did, she realised to her horror that the crown was not there. Her stomach lurched as she frantically looked around for it. She distinctly remembered setting it down beside the stream where she had first stopped, but she could not recall seeing it since then. She slumped helplessly to the ground. 'I have failed you for certain this time!' she cried. 'You should not have laid such a burden upon me. I am not to be trusted with such a task.' She closed her eyes, tears pooling under her chin and, exhausted from her journey, she passed into a deep sleep, unaware that grey shadows were approaching.

By choosing to rest in the clearing, Maela had left

herself vulnerable. But she did not care. Her hope was gone. The shadows moved closer and two dark figures were almost upon her, but Maela did not stir. Her eyes were tightly shut. 'Do not be afraid,' she heard a low voice say. 'Soon you will be with the others and then you will be safe.'

'But we must make haste,' another voice said.

Maela's hope was suddenly lifted. 'They are still alive!' Her eyes smiled beneath their lids. 'I am going to be with my family again! The men will take me to them!' Having the sensation of something pressing into her back, Maela drew in a long, deep, satisfying breath. She would be safe now.

- CHAPTER 7 -

It was dark when Maela woke, and the memory of the clearing soon returned to her, but as she looked around she could not determine where she was. She knew that she was somewhere underground and, whilst she waited for her eyes to fully adjust, she sensed something move beside her.

'So, you return to us once more, Maela, Queen of Speckled Wood.'

Maela blinked. Balorn was staring at her and she realised where she must be. 'Forgive me,' she uttered, 'for I know not of what you speak. I am Maela – just Maela.'

'Indeed,' Balorn smiled. 'Well, *just Maela*, you have had a lucky escape. If Fira and I had not found you when we did, then who knows what might have befallen you.'

'Fira?' Maela exclaimed. 'Is he here?'

'I am here.'

Maela turned and saw Fira sitting behind Balorn. He had an open wound just below his left eye. 'What happened?' she gasped.

'It matters not,' Fira replied. 'All that matters is that for now you are safe. But I fear we cannot hold the men off for much longer.'

'The men!' Maela cried. 'They know where my family are! They will take me to them! I heard them!'

Balorn fixed Maela with a quizzical look. 'When did you hear this?'

'When I was in the clearing. They are still alive! The men said that I would be safe!'

'And safe you are,' Fira said. 'But there were no men anywhere near the clearing, Maela, only Balorn and myself.'

'But ... I heard them. They said that I would soon be with the others and –'

Before Maela could finish, Balorn felt it his duty to tell her that the voices she had heard had been his and Fira's. 'I am sorry,' he added, 'for I see that you held hope in what you thought was happening. But believe me, Maela, all that the men want is to claim this land for themselves. They do not think about us, or consider that they are destroying our homes, and they certainly would not care about reuniting you with your family.'

'But, I felt them,' Maela insisted. 'They were carrying me.'

'Again, I would have to say that that was us.' Balorn gazed at Maela with sorrow in his heart as the harsh reality began to sink in.

Maela deliberately avoided his gaze, looking instead at her injured foreleg. The sight of it made her weary and she winced against the pain as she tried to move it.

She then suddenly looked up and exclaimed, 'The crown! I lost the crown! The crown of leaves is lost forever!'

'Do not burden yourself further,' Balorn's voice was reassuring, 'for the crown is safe. See! It is right here beside you.'

The crown of leaves was set upon a mound of fresh green lichen and looked no worse for wear after having endured such a traumatic journey.

Comforted by its presence, Maela returned her gaze to Balorn. 'How was it found?'

'Fira will tell you all that you wish to know,' he replied, getting to his feet. 'With regret, however, I must leave you now. My family awaits news of how you are faring.' He bowed low and graciously departed the chamber.

Maela turned to Fira. 'Did you find the crown?'

'No,' Fira shook his head. 'My dear Maela. When you left your old hollow tree you were not alone. Sirus was with you, a little way behind, but following your every move. I asked him to watch you and to report back to me if help was needed. When you reached the stream's edge he thought that you would be safe and would know to cross it. But when you set off again he realised that you had left the crown behind. Furthermore, he could see that the men were closing in on it. He managed to distract their attention, then laid the burden of carrying the crown upon himself. And a burden it was indeed. For a creature so small to carry a thing of such magnitude, and yet so delicate, is to be wondered at.

'He followed you downstream, and that is when he found you, lying with your face in the water. He raised your head as best he could so that you were free to breathe, and that is when I arrived. It wrenched at my heart to see you like that, but I had to set you on your way again. I hope that you realise that now.'

Maela nodded. 'But what happened to you?' she asked. 'How did you get that wound?'

'Ah.' Fira paused briefly, then sighed. 'The details of my affliction I will spare of you, dear Maela, but just after you had gone, the men returned, and so we had no choice but to stop them. They were close, far closer than I had first thought, and were upon us within moments. We had to act fast.

'Sirus waited in position beside the stream whilst I hid behind a tree. As the men approached, they quickly caught sight of Sirus and one of them bent down to take a closer look at him. Now, there is something you need to understand about Sirus; he is one of the wildest squirrels I know, and he pierced the man's hand so hard with his teeth that I could see the flow of blood clearly from where I stood. The man lashed out at him, but he achieved nothing more than to clip the top of Sirus's head. Sirus continued with his assault, but when the other man joined in I had to make my presence felt. And feel it they did!'

Fira paused again to gather his thoughts, but Maela, desperate to know what happened next, urged him to continue.

'My dear Maela,' Fira went on. 'How it happened, I know not, but something vast began to stir within the woodland. At first I thought that it was just the wind, but it was far greater than that. It grew in strength, chilling the air, whirling above our heads before coming down upon the men. Sirus and I stood back, feeling the effects of the cold, disbelieving what was taking place before our very eyes. I cannot explain it. It seemed to come from within the trees themselves, as though it had been summoned by their very souls.

'Driven by fear, the men made a hasty retreat and we did not see them again. But that is not to say that they will not return. For now they are sure to be curious as to what drove them away, and they will come back, in greater number no doubt.' Fira paused once more, noticing the look of bewilderment on Maela's face. 'But for now, I will speak no further of this, dear Maela, as I have already spoken more than I intended. You need to rest now, and see that your leg is healed.'

- CHAPTER 8 -

Balorn's sett went deep underground, forming an orderly network of lengthy tunnels and chambers. Maela was taken to a chamber just inside the entrance, which had been prepared with a fresh bed of dry leaves and grasses. There she lay, surrounded by extra bedding to keep her warm. For a night and a day she rested, whilst Balorn's two sisters, Belana and Baralda, tended to her needs. Using this time to think, she wondered at the strength of the wind that had driven the men away. She did not speak of it to anyone, but felt that she already knew where it had come from.

It was a comfort to Maela, being inside a real sett again, but never before had she been in one of such magnitude. After suffering the loss of her family, and finding her own modest home cruelly destroyed, she had been forced to find somewhere else to live. The old abandoned tree hollow had only meant to be somewhere to rest and shelter until she found somewhere more suitable, but it was safe and quiet in there, and she grew to like it.

Her leg healed quickly, and by the second nightfall

she felt well enough to venture outside. The cool evening air was pleasant and welcoming as she emerged unheeded, her nose held high as she sniffed her new surroundings. Balorn's sett was dug skilfully into a steep bank, sheltered beneath a canopy of ancient oak trees. A vast thicket of bramble grew just beside the entrance and Maela used this to hide behind whilst she got her bearings.

Moonlight cast a patchwork of silver between the trees, and as Maela stared into the distance, her thoughts turned to her mother. From what she had learned about her journey there, certain things that her mother had once told her were starting to make more sense. 'I realise now,' she spoke calmly, 'what it is that I must do. But I cannot do it alone. I know that you were with me on my journey here, Mother, and I can only presume that it was you who summoned the wind to assist Fira and Sirus, but I still need you with me, to guide me, and to see that I do not fail.'

'You will not fail,' came a soft voice inside her head. 'You are amongst friends now, and you must take guidance from them. I will always watch over you, my sweet Maela, and assist you whenever I can, but you must let me go. The fate that was once mine is now yours. You have learnt much these last few nights and soon you will need all your strength. But I cannot guide you now, for I myself could not see the task through that was laid before me. You will not fail, Maela. You must not fail. You cannot fail.'

The voice slowly ebbed away, leaving Maela distraught. 'I cannot let you go,' she cried. 'For if I do, then I shall surely fail! Please do not leave me, Mother. Please! Please ...' she backed further into the thicket, not caring that the hair on her back was becoming entangled in the thorns. Closing her eyes, she cried out, 'Please do not leave me!'

A short distance away, Balorn was returning from a Council meeting. He was eager to speak with Maela, and as he approached his sett, he was startled to hear her pitiful cries. Shifting his position slightly, he looked towards the thicket of bramble. 'Hullo?' he called. With no reply, and with increasing concern, he hurried around to the other side of the thicket. 'Maela? Is that you?'

Maela looked up. Tears were streaming down her face.

'What is it that troubles you?' Balorn enquired. 'Are you still in pain?'

Maela shook her head.

'Then what is it? Please, Maela, come out and talk with me. We have much to discuss.'

Balorn offered out his paw and, with great reluctance, Maela took it. She crawled out of the thicket and, after carefully removing several thorns from her hair, positioned herself awkwardly beside Balorn. She avoided his gaze and stubbornly refused his wish for her to speak.

'Very well,' Balorn sighed. 'I will speak first. It grieves me to see that you are already troubled, Maela, but I fear that I must trouble you further. I have just adjourned a Council meeting to come and speak with you. We have been discussing matters of the highest importance, most of which now greatly concerns you, and so I wish for you to come back with me and be part of the discussion. Please join us, Maela, and bring the crown of leaves with you.'

'What use am I?' Maela uttered. 'I know nothing of any matters that you discuss.'

'You know far more than you are willing to let on,' Balorn said with confidence. 'Come. For we have much to learn from each other.'

*

The Council meeting was held to the south of Balorn's sett. On the way, Balorn talked things through with Maela and filled her in on what had already been discussed. She listened to what he told her, but adamantly refused to discuss the matters on her own mind.

It was not far to walk, but Maela soon tired. Her leg

remained stiffened from her injury, but after a short rest, she managed to limp the remainder of the way, helped to some extent by an ensuing wind.

The members of the Council were assembled within a ring of slender hazel trees, waiting patiently for Balorn's return. Many of them were deeply immersed in their own conversations, discussing the matters at hand, and did not notice Balorn and Maela approach. When Fira stood up to welcome them, silence filled the air.

Balorn entered the ring and Maela followed close behind, carrying the crown in her mouth. She sat down next to Balorn, placing the crown at her side, not daring to meet another's eye until he started to introduce them.

'Here,' he gestured to Maela's left. 'This is Sirus.' The young, grey squirrel lowered his eyes and smiled. He had helped to save Maela's life, yet all she could do at that moment was return his smile, albeit half-heartedly. 'And this,' Balorn moved on to the next member, 'is Yebbut.' A large common toad nodded his head thoughtfully. 'Next is Earlan.' A sleek, male blackbird chirruped his greeting. Balorn then hesitated. Sat on the opposite side of the ring, facing him, was another fox, much older in years than Fira. 'And this,' Balorn swallowed hard, 'is Vulpash,' and before the old fox had a chance to speak, he moved on. 'And here we have Ruzig,' a long thickset adder flicked out his tongue, 'Beamer,' a scrawny tawny owl blinked, 'and One-Eyed Mas,' a curious looking brown rat offered a crooked grin. 'And finally,' Balorn looked to his right, 'Fira, who you already know.'

Maela sat tight, her paw finding the crown of leaves as a gust of wind threatened to take it.

'Members of the Council,' Balorn continued. 'This is Maela.' Upon hearing her name, all of the members bowed low. All, that is, apart from Vulpash, who chose to remain still. Only his watchful dark eyes acknowledged her presence.

'You all know why I have brought Maela here,' Balorn stood before the Council, 'and you may have noticed that she brings with her the crown of leaves.' He turned to Maela and invited her to move the crown forward so that all members could see it.

Each and every eye rested upon the crown, in awe of its presence. But one member was clearly on edge. 'We can wait no longer!' Vulpash could not believe that the time had finally come. He stood tall, turning his eyes upon Balorn. 'Chief of the Council. We cannot delay in appointing a new sovereign.'

'I quite agree,' Balorn replied. 'And that is why we are here. For too long now we have debated over who should be appointed. But the time has come, with the finding of the crown, for us to finally make a decision. King or queen, we must decide upon our new sovereign.'

'Then let us do it!' Vulpash cried impatiently. 'We are wasting precious time!'

Balorn, ignoring the outburst, turned to Maela. 'Is there anything that you wish to speak of in front of the

Council?' he asked her. But Maela did not answer. 'Maybe you would like to speak of how you came to find the crown of leaves?' Balorn urged, but still Maela held silent. 'Or maybe –'

'We should just get on and cease this idling!'

Again, Balorn ignored the fox and continued to address Maela. 'Would you care to speak with me alone?' he whispered.

Maela nodded in response, for she had already had enough of prying eyes and the harsh tones of Vulpash. She felt at unease in such situations.

'This meeting will not continue this night,' Balorn announced to the rest of the Council. 'I now have far more pressing matters to attend to.'

'Far more –?' Vulpash feigned a cough. 'What could be more pressing than to appoint a new sovereign?'

'Maela and I have much to discuss on that very matter,' Balorn spoke plainly, 'as I believe she knows far more about it than any of us here.' He offered Maela a sidelong glance.

'If she knows something, then she should share it with all of us!' Vulpash cried. Several other members nodded in agreement.

'Vulpash, please!' Balorn raised a paw to dissuade the fox from saying any more, but his attempt failed.

'I know what you are doing,' Vulpash growled. 'You are going to persuade this – this mere cub to take on the role of our sovereign. If I did not know better, Balorn, I would say that you are doing this only because she is of your kind.'

'Hold your tongue!' Balorn stiffened. 'I am still your acting leader! What then would you have me do? Appoint you?'

'I can think of none better. And if *she* had not come here, then I would have been appointed for sure.' Vulpash shot a look of pure spite at Maela.

'Is that so?' Balorn sneered.

'Yes, that is so! It is about time we had a proper leader – one whom we can trust and rely on.'

'Trust – yes!' Fira cut in, unable to let the moment pass. 'Rely on – yes! So why, then, would we want to appoint you?'

A fire burned deep behind Vulpash's eyes. 'I am surprised at you, Firana,' he scorned. 'Or maybe I did not make myself clear last time …'

From the way they were exchanging looks of pure hatred, it was clear to Maela that there was some previously unresolved history between the two foxes.

'Enough!' Balorn's harsh tone brought the Council's attention back to him. 'The role of sovereign is not up for dispute!'

'But a badger we had before!' Vulpash raged. 'We do not need another to step in and fail as her namesake did.'

'My mother did not fail!'

Maela's tenacious cry echoed through the darkness. Further and further it travelled, fading with every repetition, until it paled into insignificance, and even the wind fell silent.

- CHAPTER 9 -

Indistinct whispers began to spread through the ring like tendrils unfurling. All eyes were upon Maela and, as these whispers turned into low mutterings, Balorn knew that he had to act fast, fearing that a tumult of cries was due to erupt at any moment. He backed Maela out of the ring, passing to her the crown of leaves, before raising himself up and calling for silence.

'Friends, this meeting has already been called to an end and now you know the reason why. Go now, but be prepared to come back if I should send for you. This night is long but over.'

One by one, the Council members began to depart, each turning their gaze back towards Maela as they passed her, looking upon her as though they had only just noticed her. Some were looks of sorrow, some were of remorse. Fira and Sirus offered looks of sheer wonder and admiration. But Vulpash, the last to depart, shot a look of pure spite.

There was a stillness in the air as Maela and Balorn stood just outside of the ring of hazel trees and it was some time before Maela felt able to speak. 'Did I do wrong?' she asked. 'I did not mean to speak in such haste.'

'It was not wrong,' Balorn replied. 'You were provoked, but you did right.'

'Then why do I feel so torn inside? Look at me. I am shaking.'

'My dear Maela, I am proud of you, so do not feel torn. The truth had to be revealed and it was far better that it came from you.'

'You were not surprised though, were you?'

'I was not altogether surprised, no. My time as Leader of Speckled Wood has taught me much, not least to look for answers where none appear to lie.'

Maela's expression faltered. 'I know not what you mean.'

'Then let me explain.' Balorn sat down and gestured for Maela to do the same. 'When Fira told me of his meeting with you, and of your name, like him, I first thought that you were our queen, returned to us. But when I saw you for myself, I knew that this was not possible. However, when I heard that you had the crown of leaves, I knew then that a sign had been given to me, but also that time was not on our side. I can only presume, Maela, that you yourself did not realise until very recently the fate that lies before you, and it must have come as quite a shock. You felt alone, did you not? I have heard you speak with your mother's spirit, and I feel for you, Maela, I really do, but I must now make certain that you fully understand your task.'

'I cannot do it,' Maela objected. 'I am too young. You

are the leader now. Why can you not continue with this task?'

'Believe me, Maela, I would have done, if only to prevent Vulpash from taking on the task himself. But your presence here changes everything. You are the true heir of Speckled Wood. The crown has been passed on to you. Did your mother never tell you of such things?'

After much thought, Maela's eyes brightened. 'Oh!' she gasped. 'Yes! It was told to me in a song! My mother used to sing it to me all the time! I sang it to myself only a few days ago, but ... I have just remembered a final verse. I cannot believe that I had forgotten!'

'Do you remember the words to this verse?'

'I think so. Although it has been some time. My mother often used to leave that verse out, but I will try to remember.' And so, after a little more thought, Maela raised herself up and began to sing:

When my leaves have fallen
They must soon be found,
For her fate is bound
And upon her their beauty must then lie sound.

This woodland around me is mine.
But as night grows long
The feelings grow strong
That here in this realm we'll no longer belong.

When my leaves have fallen
I'll not see through the night.

May her future be bright,
For there has to be hope then to make the wrongs right.

Ever we dwell within man's eye.
We are put to the test
But they will not rest
Ere the day the leaves are all gone from the West.

Maela paused, staring out into the darkness, before continuing:

When my leaves have fallen
She'll be the one
To resume what's begun
And to rule over all if this land's to be won.

Balorn pondered deeply over the words. 'That indeed tells us a lot,' he said at last. 'Do you not see, Maela? You were right to say that your mother did not fail, for she has provided all that you need to carry on after her. I fear that time has been our only downfall. If news of the crown had come to us sooner, then –'

'I may not have had to leave my home.' Maela's eyes glistened. 'If the truth be known, I knew of it long before it came to Fira's eyes. The location of where I found it I am still unwilling to disclose, but it was a favourite place of my mother's that she loved to visit. It was close to our original home, but when that was destroyed, and I was forced to live elsewhere, I myself often visited that place, and soon after, I found the crown. I did not at first realise what it was, but my mother's scent was all over it, so I took care of it, knowing that it must have been hers. It was not until Fira told me of the Queen of Speckled Wood, and of the search to find her, that I realised what it must be.'

'*When my leaves have fallen ...*' Balorn pondered once more. 'Yes, meaning her crown. She foretold the future, Maela. It is up to you now to *resume what's begun* and to see that all *wrongs* are made *right*.'

'But I cannot do it,' Maela argued. 'I do not have the strength or the courage, or even the knowledge to do what my mother did.'

'I do not expect you to do it alone, dear Maela, but you must do it. I will guide you, of course, for I know much of what goes on in this woodland and together we will put an end to this fight. The creatures of Speckled Wood need someone to look up to, someone to put their hope in, and that, dear Maela, has to be you. It is your fate.'

*

Fate or no fate, Maela knew that something had to be done to protect Speckled Wood. She sat for a while, resting her head against one of the hazel trees, and thought about what Balorn had said. Her mind was an endless blur; a cloud of uncertainty and doubt, but she had to make a decision. Her options were simple: accept the challenging role of sovereign or run back home and return to a life of solitude.

In need of more time, Maela looked up, high into the canopy above her and beyond – far beyond. She found solace staring into the darkness with nothing to hinder her, and soon found herself humming the sweet melody of her mother's song again. It comforted her, and every now and again she voiced a few of the lines, remembering her mother's woeful expression when she had last sung it. As the final few words left her, she knew what she had to do.

'I'll be the one!' she cried out. 'I'll resume what's begun! I'll rule over all to see this land won!' Her voice then fell to a whisper. 'And I will do it for you, Mother. I will do it for you.' She stood tall, her mother's crown at her side.

'So, you have decided.' Balorn had not been far away. 'This is indeed great tidings!'

'I know not what is to be done,' Maela said, turning to face him. 'I have wasted much time, Balorn, but this is where my failings cease. Whatever duties need to be performed must be done this night, and that I entrust to you.'

Balorn looked upon Maela with deep admiration and with all the honour that she rightly deserved. The change in her was astounding, so much so that speech almost failed him. He bowed low. 'It shall be done.'

- CHAPTER 10 -

The preparations were made and the ceremony to appoint the new sovereign was set to begin. The moon had long since passed from view and the Council members were gathered in their usual places within the ring of hazel trees. Numerous other creatures assembled close by, all eager to witness their new queen for the first time.

Balorn's place within the ring stood empty, but for the crown of leaves, and in his absence, much discussion was taking place between the Council members

'Of course she knows of the task before her,' Fira exclaimed, 'or she would not have agreed to this!'

'*Yebbut!* It is said that she is far too young to pursue it,' the large toad argued.

'And why should that matter?' Sirus remarked. 'She is the rightful heir to the crown of leaves, is she not?'

'*Yebbut!* It is also said that she is not of sound mind and that she was forced to accept the role of our sovereign.'

'Nonsense!' Fira cried. 'You know not of what you

speak!'

'*Yebbut! Yebbut!* It is said –'

'By whom? Who has filled your head with such nonsense? And why do you listen so?'

Yebbut the toad did not reply, but a sidelong glance at Vulpash confirmed Fira's suspicions. Vulpash was staring fixedly at the crown of leaves, unaware that he was being watched. 'By rights it should be mine,' he was muttering to himself. 'What right does *she* have? *She*, who does not belong here!'

Fira continued to watch as Vulpash's eyes burned with deep desire. But just as he was about to confront him, Balorn entered the ring.

'Friends!' he called out, and immediately the woodland fell silent. 'Members of the Council! The wait is over! The time has come for our new sovereign to be crowned. Please, all rise.'

Balorn waited for the sound of rustling leaves to die down before signalling to Maela. She entered the ring, her paws trembling with every step. As she approached her place beside Balorn, avoiding the mass of staring eyes, she thought only of her mother, and pride took precedence over her nerves.

'Friends,' Balorn went on. 'Long have we waited for this moment. Since the loss of our last queen, we have lived only by our own guidance. But now her daughter, Maela, the rightful heir to the crown of leaves, has come to us, and here, before the sun rises, she shall begin her reign.' Aware of the spiteful look that Vulpash was giving him, Balorn stooped to pick up the crown. He then stood before Maela.

'Behold! The crown of leaves!' Fira exclaimed. 'The Acer Crown!' The other woodland creatures remained silent as Fira then began to recite the ancient words of the crowning ceremony. 'Creatures of Speckled Wood! You are all here to witness the crowning of our new sovereign, and in doing so you agree to be guided by her and to obey her words.'

Vulpash's eyes burned with malice.

'I ask you all now to bow and to hail! Maela, Queen of Speckled Wood!'

Balorn raised the crown and lowered it onto Maela's head. He and the other creatures then bowed low. Closing her eyes, Maela offered up a silent prayer to her mother.

When the creatures looked up again, they were in awe of their new queen who now stood before them. No longer was she weak and fearful, and full of regret. Now she was strong; her hope restored by the true faith of her mother.

*

Rays of weak autumn sunshine leached through the trees, flecking the damp woodland floor. Maela and Balorn sat together, just outside the entrance to his sett. They were quite alone, accompanied only by the distant voices of the dawn chorus, rejoicing at the coming of their new sovereign. Maela listened intently to every word that Balorn spoke to her. She wanted to know everything about Speckled Wood: every duty that needed performing, every meeting that was to be held, every idea put forward, every view held and every plan already made concerning the impending battle with man. But above all else, she wanted to learn more about the woodland creatures. Or to be more precise, about Vulpash.

'Do not concern yourself with him,' Balorn advised at length. 'Many years he has dwelt here and many attempts he has made to claim the role of sovereign for himself. But you mark my words, Maela, Queen of Speckled Wood, he would stop at nothing to be where you are right now.'

Maela shuddered at being addressed so formally. 'That will take some getting used to,' she admitted, more to herself. She then asked, 'But why is he so determined to rule?'

'Like the rest of us, he just wants to see the wrongs of this woodland put right, but, unlike the rest of us, he thinks that he can do it better. But I say again, do not concern yourself with him. He is just one more burden that you do not need.'

- CHAPTER 11 -

Maela spent her first day as Queen of Speckled Wood resting in the comfort of Balorn's sett. His two sisters prepared a special chamber for her, lined with the finest bedding they could find, and added the small bed of refreshed green lichen upon which Maela set the Acer Crown. She did not sleep, but spent her time in the deepest of thoughts, welcoming the chance to rest and to be alone once more.

Shortly before dusk, Maela began to get restless, knowing that she would soon have to face her Council members and address them for the first time. She paced the chamber floor, if only to relieve the stiffness in her leg, concerned that soon she might have to lead the woodland creatures into battle. Anxiously, she scratched at her bedding, rearranging it into a more comfortable pile, but as she settled herself back down, she felt fearfully sick. Her stomach churned. She needed fresh air.

A gentle breeze rustled through the highest branches of the towering oak trees, causing Maela's favourite leaves to cascade all around her. She loved to sit amongst the fallen leaves, and wondered whether she would ever see her old oak tree again.

Looking high into the canopy, she noticed something shifting between the branches. Her eyes followed it as it scrambled skilfully down one of the trunks and came to rest just short of where she sat.

Acknowledging her presence, Sirus bowed low.

'Oh, my dear Sirus,' Maela got to her feet. 'Whatever must you think of me?'

Sirus looked up, bewildered.

'I have not yet thanked you for saving me on my journey here. If it had not been for you, then ...'

'It was nothing,' Sirus waved the idea out of his mind.

'Nothing?' Maela frowned.

'I simply mean that there is no need for you to thank me,' Sirus explained. 'For it is I that should be thanking you. Your presence here has already changed the lives of so many creatures and you have given us all fresh hope for the future. I was only too pleased to help. I would have done anything to see you here safely.'

Maela took a step back. She had not been aware of how much the woodland creatures were relying on her and was clearly moved by Sirus's words. 'Be that as it may,' she said, 'I remain grateful for all you did.' She smiled, and with nothing more to say, Sirus bowed low and graciously departed.

The last golden rays of the setting sun faded, and Maela shivered as the breeze grew in strength. She batted a leaf away from her nose and thought again about how she was going to address her Council members. She started to piece together the beginnings of a speech, wondering what kind of a response she would get and whether she would ever have the same authority that Balorn seemed to hold over them.

Snap!

Maela spun round. 'Hullo? Is someone there?'

'You should not be out alone.' A dark figure emerged from behind the thicket of bramble. 'It is not safe for you here.'

'Vulpash!' Maela exclaimed. 'What business do you have here?'

'I was about to ask you the same question.' Vulpash stood facing Maela. 'You have no business here. It was mere chance that you came to us. This was never to be your fate.'

'May I remind you who you are talking to?' Maela raised her chin. 'I am the Queen of Speckled Wood – *your* queen – and I will not be spoken to in this manner.'

'Queen, you say? *My* queen?' Vulpash pondered for a moment, his cold eyes fixed intently on Maela. 'Ah, yes,' he went on. 'But that would mean that I would have to look up to you and obey your every command.' Maela lengthened her neck, and in response, Vulpash raised himself up to his tallest stance, looking down his long snout at her. 'If I am to look up to you, then you will have to give me a reason to. All I see before me now is a naïve young cub.'

'Hold your tongue, Vulpash! I will not be answerable

to you!'

'Your mother had much to answer for though, did she not? Or maybe you did not know. She was a coward, your mother, and ran away at the first hint of trouble.'

Maela felt the anger rise within her, burning through her veins. 'You lie!' she growled.

'Why would I lie about something as serious as that?'

'You hated my mother,' Maela cried. 'I know that, and I know why you are doing this now. You may have succeeded in grinding my mother down with your evil lies and schemes, but you will not do the same with me!'

'Evil lies? Schemes? Ah, let me guess, Balorn, our respected Chief of the Council, has been filling your mind with his own lies. He is not to be trusted. I am surprised you have not seen through him yet.'

'Enough!'

Maela and Vulpash turned. They had been joined by another.

'I have heard enough!' Fira stood between them. 'Forgive me, my Queen,' he said, bowing to Maela, 'but you would do well to go back to your chamber. I do not wish for you to see, or even hear, anything that passes between Vulpash and myself. Many quarrels we have to settle.'

Maela looked past Fira. Vulpash was scratching at a fallen branch, inspecting his claws absent-mindedly. 'I do not need you to fight my battles anymore, Fira.'

'My dear Maela, my Queen, this is not your battle. The quarrels between Vulpash and I go way back before your time. Please, take me at my word, you do not wish to be involved.'

'Fira is right.' Balorn had emerged and was looking upon Maela with deep remorse. 'This does not concern you, my Queen.'

'If it concerns the creatures of this woodland, then it concerns me,' Maela replied.

'True,' Balorn nodded. 'But just this once, trust that you would be wiser to turn your back.'

Looking between Fira and Vulpash, Maela reluctantly allowed herself to be steered away, back to the safety of her chamber.

In the fading light, Fira and Vulpash stood facing each other, neither one of them daring to make the first move. This was no ordinary quarrel. To them, this was a battle of their very own; a long-overdue battle that could not be settled by words alone.

At length, Vulpash inspected his claws again. Fira eyed him with caution, knowing that time was short, but knowing also that any sudden movement would not work in his favour.

'I am surprised at you, Firana,' Vulpash spoke at last. 'I have provided you with many an opportunity to confront me and get this *quarrel*, as you call it, settled. Up until now, I thought that maybe you had lost your nerve, but you have just shown great courage. Could it be that you now have something to prove? To Maela, maybe? Yes, that is what I first thought. But you have turned her away. Are you then scared that you will fail?'

'Your words cannot hurt me,' Fira stood his ground.

'So let us not delay.'

Their eyes met with malicious intent. Vulpash then launched himself at Fira, fixing his jaws around his opponent's throat. He scratched deep into Fira's side, tugging at his flesh, russet red fur filling the air. A mix of searing pain and determination sent their chilling screams echoing fearsomely through the woodland.

From deep within Balorn's sett, Maela could bear it no longer. 'What is it about?' she cried, looking to Balorn in desperation. 'How can you sit there and let them tear each other apart?'

'It all stems back to when your mother was crowned,' Balorn spoke with sadness in his eyes. 'The feelings that Vulpash had then are echoed in the way that he is feeling now. Fira accused him of many things – things that not even I am certain about – but neither of them will let it lie. I am only sorry that it has come to a head now, and that you are here to witness it.'

The sound of piercing screams echoed through the chamber. 'They must be stopped!' Maela cried. 'They will kill each other for certain!'

Balorn hurried from the chamber, Maela scurrying after him. What they found when they emerged outside was a horrifying scene – enough to turn even the strongest of stomachs. A trail of bloodstained leaves and scattered red fur led them to the body of Fira, lying rigid, drenched with blood, eyes closed.

- CHAPTER 12 -

Vulpash was nowhere to be seen, yet his presence was felt as Balorn stooped over Fira's body.

'Is –? Is he dead?' Anguish swelled in Maela's throat, choking her words.

'He is not dead,' Balorn replied. 'But his time here is short if we do not move him.' He looked up and scoured the surrounding woodland. There was an unusual silence that unnerved him. Vulpash was close by; his rancid scent lingering in the air. But however much he wanted to find him, and whatever he had in mind to do with him, would have to wait. Fira was his main concern.

He called to his two sisters, who set to work immediately, preparing a chamber for Fira. They arranged a plentiful mound of fresh, dry bedding, working tirelessly until they were satisfied that Fira would be comfortable. They then watched, solemnly, as his limp body was carried in.

Fira did not stir. His wounds were treated, his fur was cleaned, but his eyes remained firmly closed. One of his distant relatives – a cousin, named Famor – came to his side as soon as he heard news of Fira's affliction, but no other relatives were to be found. The sisters took it in turns to watch over Fira and to regularly report back to Maela and Balorn, but the news was always the same.

Maela could not bring herself to visit Fira. Already haunted by the image of him lying rigid on the ground, she needed no reminders. To pass the time, she paced back and forth beside the thicket of bramble; her actions making her seem more like a sentry than a queen, but she did not know what else to do.

Stopping just outside the entrance to Balorn's sett, she stared into the darkness above her. There at last she managed to lose her thoughts amongst the branches of the towering oak canopy. She imagined herself as one of the leaves, descending gently. The subtle breeze was taking hold of her, guiding her this way and that, slowly carrying her down, twisting and turning, before finally laying her to rest amongst her own kind. Closing her eyes, she drew in a long, deep breath. Somehow nothing else seemed to matter anymore.

She remained in that state for some time, losing herself in her other world, feeling safe in her new haven, until the sudden sound of laughter wrenched her cruelly back to her senses. It was a cold, heartless laugh. An unmistakeable laugh. But from which direction had it come? 'Oh yes, you can mock,' Maela cried out, flicking her eyes this way and that, 'but you will get what is due to you. I shall see to that.'

'My Queen.'

Maela turned to find Balorn bowed low behind her. 'What is it?' she breathed, noting the pained look in his eyes.

'I think you should come and see for yourself.'

A sudden, brisk wind ruffled Maela's hair, urging her to follow Balorn back into his sett. 'How is he?'

'He is extremely frail,' Balorn warned, 'but he is awake.'

The sight of Fira, lying helpless on a mound of bedding, turned Maela's stomach. She felt sick, remembering back to when she had seen him outside, and to how it could have so easily been avoided. Famor, who was sat at his side, rested a paw on his cousin's leg. 'You have another visitor.'

Fira's eyes lit up momentarily and he attempted to raise his head. 'Maela,' he choked. 'My Queen.'

'Do not tire yourself,' Famor warned. 'You need rest.' He glanced fleetingly at Maela. 'I will leave you two alone now and get some air.'

On closer inspection, Maela felt that Fira did not look so bad. His wounds were exceptionally clean, and his fur was neat, if not a little patchy in places. Taking one step closer to where he lay, she looked upon him with grave concern. 'How are you feeling?' she asked. 'I do hope you are not in too much pain.'

'You carry far too many burdens, my Queen,' Fira replied with great effort. 'I see clearly the weight of them in your eyes.' Maela stood silent, uncertain of how to respond. 'Tell me that which most burdens your heart,' Fira added.

'How did it come to this?' Maela stalled for something more positive to say. 'This should never have happened. Maybe if you had not found me, then –'

'What?' Fira cut in. 'I would not have come to know the kindest, most beautiful creature in this woodland – that is for certain. And you would not have come into power.' He paused briefly, noticing a curious change in Maela's expression. 'But I see now what burden's you most,' he lowered his eyes. 'Do not blame yourself, my Queen. None of this is your fault.'

'But I could have done something to stop it,' Maela protested. 'I should have done something – anything in my power to prevent such a thing happening.'

'Your concerns should now be with saving Speckled Wood. Your power is needed elsewhere.'

'But what power have I against man?'

'My dear Maela, my Queen, do you not remember my words when we first met? I told you that there are ways to fight man. But what I did not tell you was that only the sovereign has the power to do so.' Maela stared at Fira with desolate eyes. 'And so I wonder,' Fira went on, 'whether you recall seeing a group of gnarled old trees near to the stream where you fell?'

'Gnarled trees?' Maela frowned. 'Twisted trees?'

'Yes,' Fira nodded. 'Those are the Coil Trees, and they are ancient, having dwelt here in this woodland far longer than any other of their kind. They hold a power of their very own, but only the ruler of Speckled Wood holds any power over them.'

Maela's eyes widened. 'The wind!' she exclaimed. 'A

chilling wind came out of the trees and drove the men away! That is what you told me!'

'Indeed I did. But that was no ordinary wind that Sirus and I witnessed. I pretended at the time not to know what it was, for your sake Maela, but the truth must now be told.' Fira paused for a moment, seemingly in deep thought. 'The Coil Trees possess earthly spirits,' he began to explain, 'spirits that are kept deep within their roots. The wind was simply the release of those spirits, meant only as a warning to see the men off. It was not at its full strength by any means. But know this, dear Maela, the power of the Coil Trees is precious, and is only to be employed when the woodland is under threat. If it is misused or abused in any way, then the spirits will turn, and will most likely destroy anything and everything around them.'

Fira swallowed hard, giving Maela the chance to think this through, before continuing. 'But what I cannot understand,' he said, 'is how the spirits were released when we were without a sovereign.'

Maela hesitated, then told Fira of the recent conversations between her and her mother's spirit. 'The wind must have been summoned from her,' she concluded.

Fira's strength was waning, but he managed to smile with compassion. 'Yes. That makes sense to me. The Coil Trees were always so kind to your mother when she was queen, so I can only wonder at their joy at being summoned by her spirit.' He allowed his eyes to close before emitting a short, sharp cough.

'You need rest,' Maela told him.

'As do you,' Fira replied, his eyes half opening.

'No time for that,' came the sound of Balorn's voice. He appeared at the chamber entrance. 'My Queen,' he bowed, 'we can delay no longer. Beamer has just informed me that at the first light of day, men will return to the West, and in far greater numbers. We have to be ready.'

Maela appeared forlorn, looking back at Fira. 'It seems I must now leave,' she told him. 'But I will remember what you told me. And if I can assure you that nothing will go wrong on my part, then that at least may bring comfort to you.'

'It does, my Queen. It does.'

With a heavy heart, Maela turned to leave, wondering whether this was to be their final parting. But she had gone no further than the chamber entrance when she heard Fira's voice again. 'May the spirit of your mother be with you, Maela, my Queen. Look to her for guidance and do not ever look back.'

Maela did not look back, but instead found herself staring into the desperate eyes of Balorn.

'I wish you well,' Fira added finally.

'And I you.'

- CHAPTER 13 -

There was a noticeable change in the air when Maela emerged from the sett. It was as though the entire woodland had transformed into a pit of despair, with the only hope of survival resting on Maela's young shoulders. Balorn followed her out, carrying with him the crown of leaves. He placed it at her feet, then shuddered, having also noticed the change. 'This is to be a long night,' he remarked, gazing far into the distance. 'But we must prevail. We have to prevail if this land is to be won.'

'And what of Fira?' Maela asked.

'Famor will remain with him, and my sisters will see that he is taken care of. Please, do not burden yourself further, my Queen. We have much to prepare for.'

Every creature in the woodland that was able to fight was called upon to assemble at Grey Stone Pond, just to the west of Balorn's sett. A vast crowd had already gathered by the time Maela and Balorn arrived, and Maela gazed in awe at the bravery of the creatures prepared to go into battle to save their homes.

Balorn signalled for quiet. 'Friends, this is indeed a

grave night. But let us not forget that it is also a time to rejoice! For once again, power has been restored to us and we must now look to our queen for guidance.'

A few individuals began to cheer at hearing these words, but it was not the joyous reaction that Balorn had hoped for.

'My friends,' he went on, 'I speak of course of the great power and that of the trees. Come, my friends, and rejoice! Let us now put all our hope and trust in our queen!'

A tumult of elated voices erupted from the crowd and Balorn shouted above them, 'Hail! Maela, Queen of Speckled Wood!'

As his words resounded through the darkness, Balorn turned to Maela and set the Acer Crown upon her head. His eyes willed her to address the crowd, but despite all her preparations, Maela could not bring herself to do it. 'There is nothing left to say,' she told him. 'You have already said all that they needed to hear.'

'They still need words of encouragement,' Balorn urged. 'That is all. Just a few words. You have nothing to fear.'

Several voices within the crowd continued to cheer, but soon their focus was on Maela. Forcing herself to stand tall, she breathed in the atmosphere, giving the impression that she was calm and completely at ease. She then raised her head high. 'We are put to the test!' she exclaimed. 'But we will not rest! We must go on to the West! To the West!

'To the West!' came the resonant reply.

'Friends!' Balorn raised a paw, calling for silence. 'Before we begin, you should know that for part of the journey we shall be travelling in two groups. Queen Maela and I will divert our path, together with Sirus, One-Eyed Mas and Beamer, whilst the rest of you continue heading west.'

The sound of someone clearing their throat turned everyone's attention to the centre of the crowd. 'If I might interject,' Vulpash raised himself up. 'Are we to have a leader?'

Balorn glared at the fox. How dare he stand there, seemingly unscathed when Fira was so brutally injured? 'But of course,' Balorn did well to remain calm. 'I was about to say –'

'Then may I be so bold as to elect myself for the position?'

With time being so short, and with no sign of objection, Balorn felt he had little choice than to accept the fox's proposal. 'So be it.' He issued Maela with a sidelong glance, hinting for her approval, but she simply signalled that the time had come.

'To the West!'

The crowd began to depart, full of fresh hope and elation, determined to succeed. Before Balorn joined them, he took Maela aside. 'I may live to regret this,' he said, more to himself.

'As long as you live, then no harm will be done.'

Balorn nodded graciously. 'I believe that Fira has filled you in on what needs to be done?'

'He has. But there is just one thing that –' before Maela could finish, a rustling of leaves behind her caused her to start. She turned to find the figure of Famor, bowed low, with something hanging from his teeth. He dropped it at Maela's feet. 'Forgive me for startling you,' he said, 'but I bear a gift from Fira. He did not want his Queen to leave without it.'

Maela glanced down. It was the ring of small alder cones that she had presented Fira with. 'Thank you,' she choked. 'And thank Fira for me also.'

'I will,' Famor nodded, 'when I return.'

'Return?' Maela quizzed Famor as to his meaning.

'I am to fight with you,' he explained.

'But this is not your fight. You do not dwell in Speckled Wood.'

'No, but Fira does. And if he thinks it is worth fighting for, then that is good enough for me.'

'Have you spoken of this with Fira?'

'I have. And he is in agreement. I shall be honoured to fight alongside any friend of his.'

'Then your presence will be most welcome.' Maela accepted the gift and attached the ring to her left foreleg. It would serve as a reminder of her recently healed injury and of when Fira and Sirus had come to her rescue.

After joining the tail end of the crowd, Maela, Balorn and Famor started their journey at a strong, steady pace. Many of the creatures were grouped together with their own kinds. The birds, who flew on ahead, made sure that the way forward was clear, and the insects, who swarmed around the perimeter of the crowd, kept everyone together. It was a sight to be wondered at, and Maela, for one, could not believe that her presence had prompted such an immediate action.

They followed a direct route, staying deep within the woodland, and Maela could not help but listen in to some of the conversations around her. Emotions were undoubtedly high, and the majority of the woodland creatures were jubilant that action was finally being taken to save the woodland. However, there were some that felt that more could have been done, and that this attempt to take on the destructive forces of man was too little too late.

Maela turned to Balorn. 'What would have happened if I had not come here?'

'It is best that you do not think about that at this time, my Queen.'

But thinking was all that Maela could do. She had so many unanswered questions scrambling through her mind that she could hardly keep track of them.

At length, the creatures entered a clearing and, under Balorn's instruction, they paused to rest. 'Friends, this is where we must part,' he announced, coming amongst the crowd. 'Once you are rested, you will continue your journey to the West and we shall meet with you after we have taken the Queen's Path.'

The Queen's Path? This was news to Maela, and she wondered again at how much Balorn and Fira were neglecting to inform her of. Looking around, she also wondered at the clearing in which she now stood, and soon recognised it to be the same one that she had found herself in on her previous journey.

As the majority of the crowd continued on the direct path, Maela, Balorn and their three followers took a different path, heading north-west.

'I remember taking this path,' Maela whispered to Balorn as they weaved their way between the densely packed trees.

'I feared as much,' he replied. 'But you should never have taken this path alone. No one, not even the sovereign, should ever take this path alone. The group of ancient trees that we are heading towards already know of our coming, so we must be on our guard. I presume that Fira told you of the powers they hold?'

'Yes, he did. But he also told me that, as Queen, I now hold a power over them.'

'That you do, my Queen. But they do not know you, and you have yet to show your authority over them. If you would allow me to give you just one piece of advice, then it would be to keep your mind clear of any misgivings. The spirits will pick up on your negativity and as a result they will not come to your aid.'

'But Balorn, I know not how to –'

'My Queen,' Balorn whispered. 'We must be quiet now. Look, there is the stream. We are getting close.'

- CHAPTER 14 -

The path began to get narrower until single file was all that could be managed. With Maela taking the lead, Balorn followed close behind, with Sirus and One-Eyed Mas bringing up the rear. Beamer flew just overhead, but found it difficult to keep up as he was forced lower under the canopy. The strange, twisted trees were entwining, closing in on one another.

Aside from the trickling stream, the woodland stood in silence. An ominous feeling blanketed the air, and a cool breeze began to scout amongst the fallen leaves. Maela could not withstand such silence, nor could she put aside the dread set deep within her stomach. The path before her appeared treacherous, but she had to continue.

Desperate to remain in positive thought, she recited her mother's song to herself, over and over in her mind, and soon found that new words were coming to her. Before long, she began to piece together her own version of the song:

Now that your leaves have fallen
Your fate lies with me

Though I did not see
Ere the day I left my old oak tree.

Our homeland I left to the men.
But they will not rest –
I'll return to the West
And summon again that which they still have not guessed.

I know that your leaves have fallen
But I call upon you
Now, to see this one through
And to send forth the wind that I know lies in you.

Maela stopped and looked behind her. She was quite alone. Balorn and the other creatures were nowhere to be seen. The only sound she could hear now was the pounding of her heart, echoing through the stillness.

A cruel, chilling wind rose up from within the trees. Leaves scattered as it grew in strength, whistling around her, encircling her, freezing her very soul, faster and faster.

'What has become of me?' Maela's eyes streamed as

the icy wind ripped through her. She caught her breath, trying to fight it, but to no avail. She could not move. The wind began to subside, leaving Maela frozen, stone-like, alone amid the scattered leaves, until a cold voice spoke to her through the darkness.

Never alone should you pass through here.
Never, unless you hold no fear.

Maela, our queen, we hear that you are,
But you are not Maela we know from afar.

Speak now and speak freely, but do not delay,
Or soon you'll regret ever coming this way.

Stricken with fear, Maela attempted to speak, but her mouth was so dry that all she could manage was a high-pitched squeak.

What language is this? I have heard of it not.
Speak up and speak clearly, or have you forgot?

'I ... I am Maela, Queen of Speckled Wood, and I come here to seek your help.'

Help is a gift we do not freely share,
Unless it's invoked by the Crown's rightful heir.

'But that is me!' Maela implored. 'I am the Crown's rightful heir. See! I wear it upon my –' she realised to her horror that she was no longer wearing the crown. 'Where is it?' she cried out, finding her voice at last. 'What have you done with it?'

The Acer Crown is with its own kind.
The leaves of my tree now have it entwined.

'What right do you have to steal my crown? I demand that you return it to me!'

To demand of the Coils proves you have strength,
But do not lose it now; you will need it at length.

We hear you have power, but our queen is not you,
So I must tell you now that your time here is through!

The wind gathered in strength and encircled Maela at a terrifying speed before rising up and disappearing into the canopy.

Maela was left reeling. 'Come back! Come back!' But her cries were in vain. Alone and bewildered, she slumped forward and covered her eyes with her paws. The ring of alder cones rubbed against the side of her head, prompting her to think of Fira. 'Oh, what have I done? I have lost my way, I have lost my friends and I have lost my crown. Must I also lose hope?'

'Hope remains with you,' came a soft, familiar voice inside her head.

'Mother?'

'My sweet Maela. I return to you now for I see that I

have failed you. Open your eyes, Maela, open your eyes.'

'You have never failed me, Mother.' Maela raised herself up again and squinted through the darkness. 'Where are you?'

'I am right here beside you, Maela. But do not look for me.' Maela's eyes flicked blindly this way and that. 'You must listen now to what I say. You have learnt much about being Queen, and I am indebted to Balorn and Fira for what they have told you. I only wish I could have done more myself, but my time spent with you must only be when you are in most desperate need. I am trying to apologise, dear Maela, as I should have made one thing much clearer to you.'

'And what is that?'

'The one thing that would have prevented your situation now.'

Maela listened intently to her mother's instruction. She then raised her head high and shouted at the top of her voice: 'Run! Run like fire!'

Without delay, the chilling wind returned and encircled Maela once again, but this time she held little fear. In front of her, and all around her, tiny wisps of light flickered as the spirits of the trees awakened. The wind then died down and the cold voice spoke.

Gather, my spirits, our queen is in need.
She calls to us now to take on the deed.

Give back to her crown and friends at no cost,
And restore to her time that she thought she had lost.

At once, the mass of wispy spirits accumulated to become one immense, forceful wind. Flecked with dancing light, it rose up in front of Maela, chilling the air in her lungs. She watched its mesmerising form as it twisted and coiled above her, until she lost all trace of time. Her trust remained firmly with her mother, yet her hope was now with the wind. She gasped and closed her eyes against the force of the wind as it started its terrifying decent. Closer it came, gathering speed, whirring hypnotically. Holding her breath, Maela dug her sharp claws deep into the frozen ground.

The wind passed straight through her, or so she believed. Shivering and dazed, Maela dared to open one eye. The familiar trickle of the nearby stream brought comfort to her and, at first glance, she appeared to be standing in exactly the same place as before. But then, as she opened the other eye and sniffed at the air, she knew that she was no longer alone.

- CHAPTER 15 -

Balorn studied Maela curiously, wondering why she had come to a sudden halt. 'My Queen,' he whispered. 'Do not linger.'

Maela spun round, wide-eyed.

'What is it, my Queen? We cannot delay?'

Engulfed with fear, Maela could not think straight, bemused by the events that had just taken place. She shook herself briskly to clear her thoughts and in doing so dislodged the crown from her head. It fell to the ground beside her. 'My crown!' she gasped.

Dutifully, Balorn picked it up and set it back upon Maela's head.

Maela gazed at him woefully. 'How long have you been here?' she breathed. 'How much time have I wasted?'

'We have only just stopped.' Balorn was wary of Maela's behaviour, but tried to make her see that time should not be wasted and that she should employ her power without delay.

'I have already done it.' Maela believed this to be true, despite an element of doubt that was creeping in.

'But that is not possible,' Balorn argued.

In that moment, the air turned bitterly cold and a sudden gust of wind took the creatures by surprise. It grew steadily more powerful, whistling through the trees, forcing Beamer to land in an undignified heap beside One-Eyed Mas.

'It seems I misjudged you, my Queen,' Balorn bowed.

Maela shuddered as a cold voice loomed out of the darkness.

We are gathered, Queen Maela, we come to your call
To take on the danger about to befall.

Rest easy, Queen Maela, we'll do all we can
To end the destruction that's brought on by man.

So lead us, Queen Maela, to us you're our guide,
But do not delay as time's not on your side.

It appeared to Maela that none of the other creatures heard the voice apart from her, but that they all knew what the wind signified. Seemingly undeterred by its presence, the group continued on their journey.

Staying close to the stream's edge, Maela and Balorn took the lead whilst the others followed on as before. Beamer spread his wings and took flight with extreme caution, not wishing to be caught by the icy wind pursuing him.

The rocky path began to clear and Maela noticed that the stream was becoming wider. It was then that she remembered having been there before. 'How are we to cross it?' she asked.

'We use the bridge,' Balorn replied, trying not to sound conceited. He diverted Maela's gaze towards a thicket of scrub growing on either side of the stream.

Bridge? Maela wondered. She edged towards the thicket and watched in awe as a small wooden structure began to appear in front of her. It stretched effortlessly across the stream, piece by piece, as though an invisible force were uncovering it.

'I did not notice this before,' she told Balorn.

'That is what I feared.'

Once each of the creatures had crossed to the other side of the stream, Maela looked back towards the thicket. The bridge was no longer visible and the thicket itself appeared much smaller, almost insignificant. Maela squinted and strained her eyes, but it was as though her entire perception of the area had changed.

Noting her reaction, Balorn brought Maela's attention back to the journey ahead of them. 'Sometimes,' he whispered, 'we can only see what is shown to us. But the truth – the reality – is often much harder to see.'

*

The moon was high above the group as they entered a more open part of the woodland. Now that they were heading west again, Maela began to feel comforted as every step was leading her back to her homeland. There was still a fair distance to travel, but they were due to meet up with the rest of the crowd soon, and Maela felt that joining forces again would make the journey more bearable.

At length, Beamer spotted the large crowd just up ahead and the sight of them came as a great relief to Balorn. But, as they approached, Vulpash could be seen standing in the centre with all the creatures gathered around him, listening to what he was saying.

Balorn immediately thought the worst. 'This cannot be good,' he told Maela as they hastened their approach. 'No doubt he is trying to put forward his own plans for how the battle should be fought. I shall rue this bitterly.'

'It matters not, Balorn. Look!'

The creatures that had been so closely gathered around Vulpash were starting to disperse. Birds and insects were flapping their wings in disgust. Other creatures were waving their limbs or thrashing their tails, turning away. Only Vulpash and Yebbut remained where they were.

'Why do they not see sense?' Vulpash shook his head in disbelief. 'They are fools if they think that Balorn's plan will work. It is clear that he has not thought this through.'

'*Yebbut*! Time is against us,' the toad argued, 'and it is the only plan we have. And they are only backing him because of the queen.'

'And what does *she* know? She knows nothing of battles; least of all how to win one.'

'*Yebbut*! She is our queen and we have to now put our trust in her.'

'Have to?' Vulpash sneered. 'My! How you've changed. Is it so that you will also turn your back on me?'

'*Yebbut! Yebbut*! It is not because I think you are wrong in putting your ideas forward, more that you are doing it the wrong way.'

'Wrong? *Wrong?*' Vulpash was exasperated. 'Does nobody here see the danger that we are in? We are not going to win this fight purely by strength in numbers! Half the creatures here are powerless against man!'

'*Yebbut!* That is what I mean. You did not have to tell them so.'

'Of course I did,' Vulpash spat. 'They needed to know, otherwise what hope is there?' A shiver ran through his spine as an icy wind swarmed the surrounding area.

'There is always hope,' came a calming voice behind him.

Vulpash spun round. 'Oh, you think so, do you?' He looked past Maela to see the other creatures gathering once more in the presence of their queen. He narrowed his eyes at Balorn, then at Sirus, then back at Maela. 'I do not see it,' he said. 'I do not see where hope could possibly lie. It is folly to continue.'

The entire crowd stared at him, making him see that he was wasting his time.

In desperation, he turned to Famor. 'It seems your cousin had the right idea,' he said through a wry smile. 'He saw that there was no hope – he told me so – and now he is lying down and taking it easy whilst the rest of us risk our lives.'

Famor lunged forward. 'You take that back!' he growled. 'You do not deserve to be here. If I had my way I would –'

'What?' Vulpash cut in. 'You would do what? Oh, I daresay I am very fortunate that you do not have your own way, but until my queen tells me otherwise, I stay. Maybe then you should ask her why she has not already told me to leave.'

All eyes fell on Maela, but she was not to be outdone. 'You stay, Vulpash, because I need you,' she said, and all those who heard her stood amazed. 'Yes,' she continued in a dreamlike manner. 'I have done much thinking on my way here and I have decided that we need a slight change of plan – a change that involves you, Vulpash, acting as a decoy.'

'A decoy?' Vulpash uttered. 'You – you mean – to use me as bait? Is that what you are saying?'

'Indeed,' Maela replied. 'It is a position of the highest regard, and I can think of no one better to take it on. However, if you do not feel you are up to it, then ...'

'No! I will do it!' Vulpash exclaimed. He noticed several creatures in the crowd mocking him. 'Oh, yes,' he jeered, 'you can all laugh. But it will be me who gets the greatest praise for taking on such a pivotal role once the battle is won!'

'That's the spirit!' Balorn cried. He urged Maela to continue addressing the crowd with her new plan, and as she did, the arrogant expression on Vulpash's face slid gradually into one of deepest despair. The plan, everyone agreed, was fool proof. Only time would tell otherwise.

- CHAPTER 16 -

After ensuring that everyone fully understood what was required of them, the short journey to Maela's homeland continued, spurred on by the impatient icy wind. The creatures ventured in a south-westerly direction and at length they came to rest beside the part of the stream that Maela knew well. It filled her with heart-warming joy to lay eyes upon it again, and she longed to go to her mother's secret place nearby. As far as she could tell from quickly surveying the area, everything was still as she had left it, but there was another place, further north, that was calling to her. She desperately wanted to see her old hollow oak tree, to know that it had survived, but she would have to wait.

Daylight would soon be upon them and already a faint mist was starting to spread throughout the woodland. Much to Balorn's relief, the icy wind died down and dispersed into the surrounding trees. 'This will be a grave day,' he whispered to himself.

Maela watched as he began to scratch at the fallen leaves before him. 'What are you thinking, Balorn?' she asked.

Shaking off his thoughts, Balorn looked up at his queen, and for the first time noticed how innocently beautiful she looked. 'I was thinking of home,' he said at last, 'and how I should miss it if it were gone. Only now do I understand how you must feel about this place. Your homeland remains always a part of you.'

'That it does,' Maela replied. 'And that is why we must defend it and do all we can to stop man needlessly destroying it.'

Hearing this, Vulpash stepped forward. 'Then why do we delay?'

Maela turned to face him. 'You already know what you are to do,' she growled, 'so I suggest you go and do it. Your first position is over there.' She gestured to a large beech tree due north of where they now stood.

Vulpash regarded her tone with displeasure, but took his leave nonetheless and scurried towards the tree. Once he was in position, Maela faced the waiting crowd. Numerous eyes stared back at her. 'You all know why we are here,' she said with authority. 'So let us delay no longer. Speckled Wood is ours! Let us use it!'

At the first sign of dawn, not a creature was to be seen, yet they were there, waiting; waiting without motion, waiting with a mix of terror and anxiety, waiting with their senses alert for the slightest hint of danger. The air was cold, far colder than it should have been for the time of year. The presence of the icy wind within the trees did nothing to stem this.

All was quiet. No dawn chorus was to be heard this day. Only the leaves dared to break the stillness as they cascaded through the branches before settling on the damp woodland floor. With every falling leaf, the tension in the air grew stronger, and with it came the ominous feeling that danger would encroach all too soon.

The mist thickened and lingered malevolently, threatening to impede Maela's plan. She watched, curiously, as every now and again, the wind within the trees silently consumed part of the mist as though annoyed at its presence. The stillness was unnerving and, like many of the creatures around her, Maela was becoming restless. She could see Vulpash scratching absent-mindedly at the beech tree's smooth trunk, but just as she was about to call to him, the silence was broken.

A low thud, as though metal had struck wood. A whistle in the distance. Then men's voices, deep and full of malice, mingled with the low monotonous thump of heavy boots. The creatures looked around them, this way and that, momentarily uncertain of what they should do. Balorn turned to Maela. 'My Queen?'

The icy wind remained calm, resisting the urge to unleash its power as Maela listened intently to the voices. 'The West!' she exclaimed suddenly, standing tall. 'Look to the West! That is where they are coming from.'

All eyes turned to look, but only the mist and the faint outlines of the trees could be seen. Vulpash, however, being slightly closer, declared, 'They are there! Look! Do you not see?' The voices and heavy footsteps grew louder, and shadowlike figures began to emerge before him. 'There are six,' he whispered as loud as he dare. 'No, wait ... seven! There are at least seven men! Do you not see?'

At that moment, it hit home to Maela just how close she had come to getting caught by the men only a few days before. This was it. The time had come. But how were they ever going to prevail against such a strong number of men? They had only planned for an attack on three, maybe four men at the most, but this changed everything. Balorn, once again, urged Maela to take control and to give Vulpash his signal to proceed.

The men, dressed in dark clothing and thick, dirty boots, stopped just short of the large beech tree behind which Vulpash was hiding. All but two of them stooped to the ground as though searching for something. Vulpash looked to Maela in desperation.

Very well, she thought to herself. *It is now or never.* Snatching a glance at the ring of alder cones on her foreleg, her thoughts turned to Fira, and with renewed determination, she raised her head high and gave Vulpash the nod.

Whilst most of the men remained distracted on the ground, Vulpash passed the group with ease. He moved with extreme stealth, causing no sound to be made, until he reached his second position. Behind the cover of another beech tree, he had a clearer view of what the men were doing. He witnessed tools of all kinds spread out on the ground before them. Tools with sharp, serrated edges and blades of all sizes. Tools with long wooden handles and blunt metal ends. Small tools that Vulpash could only wonder at their purpose. The men were sorting through them, checking them and dividing them amongst the group.

Satisfied that he had seen enough, Vulpash gave the all clear nod back to Maela. This she echoed, and that was now his command that battle should at last commence.

Leaping out from behind the tree, Vulpash emitted a terrifying bark. The men that were stooped fell awkwardly to the ground, their limbs flailing. The other two stared in stunned silence at the fox's bared teeth. Scrambling to their feet, the men started to back away. One of them laid his hands upon a spade, more by luck than judgement, and raised it to his shoulder. 'It's all right,' he breathed. 'We're not going to hurt you.'

Vulpash stood his ground, sneering with vicious

intent. A wave of panic then swept through the woodland. The sound of metal hitting the ground reverberated through the trees. Vulpash felt the force of it as he fled the scene, and with a daring glance back over his shoulder, he saw three of the men giving chase.

Maela stood silent, her eyes locked onto Vulpash's position. He was leading the men away and this was her signal. She sent out a bark of her own, which rang distinctly through the trees. The creatures of the woodland sprang out of hiding and immediately began their assault on the remaining four men.

Launching himself from a high branch, Ruzig landed with precision upon the shoulders of one of the men. Several other snakes joined in and the man fell into a quivering heap on the ground. Whilst he struggled to break free, another man fell beside him. He was smothered from head to foot with every kind of insect, biting and stinging every part of him they could find. One-Eyed Mas took command of the rodents and leapt upon the next two men. Biting, scratching and whipping their tails, they soon had them on the ground.

It was now the turn of the birds to launch their attack and to see that the men stayed down. Beamer took the lead, and with the help of jays and jackdaws, woodpeckers and magpies, he circled menacingly above the trees. The snakes, insects and rodents swiftly departed as the birds swooped down with terrifying speed. The men were surrounded; ferocious wings flapping in their faces, sharpened beaks jabbing their skin.

Confident that all was going to plan, Maela and Balorn took their leave and headed further west to where the next stage of the plan was due to take place. The mist had almost disappeared, but in places its unearthly presence lingered, slowing their journey. They stayed close to the stream, but after only a short distance, Maela came to a sudden halt.

'What is it, my Queen?' Maela's eyes were fixed, and Balorn could see that she was muttering something under her breath. 'My Queen?' he asked with more urgency.

'My trees,' Maela breathed. 'My beloved trees. They have fallen. Look what they have done.'

- CHAPTER 17 -

Where there once had stood an abundance of beech and oak, less than half now remained, with only stumps and strewn branches to show for the rest.

Balorn hung his head. 'I am sorry, my Queen, truly I am, but we cannot linger. We must move on.'

Maela continued to hold her gaze. 'Look, Balorn!' she gasped. 'Look!'

'I know, my Queen, but we must make haste.'

'No!' Maela cried. 'Look, *there!*'

Glinting a short distance in front of where they stood, a metal object was swinging to and fro. Through the mist, it appeared first on one side of a tree trunk, then on the other, returning back and forth, back and forth ...

'What do you suppose it is?' Maela kept her eyes fixed.

'I do not know,' Balorn replied. 'It is like nothing I have ever seen before.' He raised his nose high into the air. 'It does not feel safe,' he said at length. 'We should turn back.'

They were about to retreat when the faint bark of a

fox resounded through the trees. The swinging object stopped and vanished from sight. 'Now I'll 'ave you,' came a deep, growling voice from behind the thickset tree.

Maela and Balorn froze. They should never have been this close to man, especially one that was armed. The swinging metal object came into view once more, revealing itself to be the head of an axe. The man behind the tree was holding it steady, biding his time.

Another bark sounded and the distinct figure of Vulpash could be seen running on the horizon, his ears laid flat against the back of his head. He was heading directly towards the man with the axe.

Maela and Balorn had to think fast. As Vulpash ran closer, pursued by the other two men, the man behind the tree held the axe aloft, ready to strike.

'Follow my lead,' Maela whispered.

The sound of heavy footsteps was upon them all too soon, but Maela was determined. She stamped tenaciously upon a long twig, causing it to snap. Again and again she did this, stamping harder and harder until the man with the axe turned.

Alarmed at seeing two badgers so close to him, the man raised his axe higher and took a poorly aimed swing. Maela and Balorn scrambled backwards, then ran as the man raised his axe once more. Anger, mingled with frustration, was alive in his eyes; he had no intention of missing this time. He lunged towards the badgers, but as he swung the axe down, a terrifying scream gave rise to his second misjudgement. Before he could turn, he collapsed in a heap on the ground; a searing pain piercing his right leg.

Cries of agony rang through the woodland as the man kicked ferociously at his assailant. The fox's jaws were clamped around his leg, its teeth sunk deep into his flesh. The other two men, much younger in years, staggered onto the scene, breathless, but their chase was not over. Their presence prompted Vulpash to release his victim, and he ran after Maela and Balorn.

'Get 'im!' the old man seethed.

Vulpash could see the two badgers just ahead of him, leading him back the way they came. He threw a cautious glance over his shoulder and saw the two young men gaining on him. The old man was also back on his feet, axe in hand.

As Maela and Balorn neared their original positions, the air turned as thick as ice. The other four men were right in front of them, but no longer were they suppressed to the ground. Standing with their backs together in an outwards-facing ring, they were thrashing their arms frantically, brandishing whatever they had to defend themselves with. All around them, birds, insects, rodents and snakes were doing their best to keep the men at bay.

Earlan spotted Maela and issued a call to warn of the approaching danger.

Maela cried out at the top of her voice 'Run! Run like fire!'

The surrounding trees began to wake from their slumber. A faint mist exuded from their trunks, swirling forth, billowing, until the woodland was once again concealed within its presence. Maela and Balorn darted skilfully between the trees, guided only by their sense of smell, calling for the rest of the creatures to follow them. Soon, all were gathered once again beside the stream.

'That – was too close!' Sirus gasped, flicking his tail indignantly.

All the creatures could do now was wait.

The mist was rising, growing in stature, gliding stealthily westward. The group of men halted at its eerie presence, then, terrified, started to retreat. The man with the axe caught up with them, but it was too late.

From the safety of the stream, the woodland creatures watched in awe as the mist, now flecked with tiny wisps of light, began to encompass the men. Chilling cries of pain and confusion could be heard above the ever-increasing rush of the wind as it continued to billow. Then, amid the cries and screams of the men, came the unmistakeable scream of a fox.

Maela scanned the crowd around her. '*Vulpash!*' she gasped. She darted towards the mist, following its trail as another piercing scream ripped through the air.

'Maela!' Balorn ran after her, his thick, silvery hair laid flat against his back as the wind repelled him. 'My Queen!' he called. 'Come back!' He managed to grab her flank and fought to hold her back from the swirling mist. 'My Queen, there is nothing you can do!'

'But we cannot leave him!' Maela struggled to twist herself free from Balorn's grasp.

'That is exactly what we must do.'

'But he will not survive!'

Balorn looked long at Maela. Her ruffled hair gave her a despondent look, of one who had lost all hope. 'He knew the risk, my Queen.'

Maela ceased her struggle and Balorn released his grip. The mist was spiralling upwards, gaining in strength, stretching with ever-increasing ferocity towards the canopy of the trees. 'There is nothing more to be done,' Balorn choked, feeling the force of the wind upon him. 'Please, my Queen. We must go back.' He turned to leave, confident that Maela would follow him, but her eyes remained fixed upon the mist as it hovered above the ground.

The boots of seven men were clearly visible, gathered together, hanging limp. Maela watched, mesmerised, as the tiny wisps of light danced within the mist. Several patches of russet-red fur then caught her eye, scattering, spiralling to the ground before her.

'Vulpash!' Without thinking, Maela lurched forward.

Aware of her presence, a cold voice loomed through the encircling wind.

Maela, our Queen, do you hold no fear?
Get back to your friends, for danger is near.

We know why you've come. Is your faith in us lost?
For we've promised to give all help at no cost.

The one that you seek is now safe from all harm
And we'll see him returned to you once we are calm.

Maela squinted through the mist, standing as close as she dare. 'Is he –?' she choked. 'Is he –?'

We know what you wish for. We know what you please.
Get back now, Queen Maela. Return to the trees!

'Maela!' Balorn shouted. 'My Queen! Why do you delay?' He attempted to edge towards her.

'Get back!' she shouted in response. 'Everyone, get back!'

A small group of curious creatures had already left the safety of the crowd, eager to see what was happening.

'Get back!' Maela repeated more urgently. 'Take to the trees!' She ran back towards them, the icy wind ruffling her hair, urging her on to safety. Balorn ran with her, and as soon as they were a safe distance away they took refuge behind the nearest tree. They then watched in awe as the mist within the wind turned the most violent shade of blue, spinning faster and faster. It grew more powerful with every resolution, then an almighty roar like thunder burst forth through the trees, making the ground tremble.

You are not welcome. You will not return.
We will not allow you to chop down and burn.

This woodland belongs to the creatures you've seen.
Their homes now destroyed in the places you've been.

Release your weapons! Open your eyes!
The light of my spirits will tell you no lies.

From somewhere within the mist, the distinct sound of metal falling upon metal could be heard. The tiny wisps of light flickered and sparked before an explosion of blue light caused its onlookers to turn away. Twisting and coiling, the blinding mist spun, and from deep within it emitted a sound as though it was drawing in a long, cooling breath.

As cold as ice, blinded with fear,
You will not bear witness to what you've seen here.

You will never remember these words that I say,
As far from this woodland we take you away!

The encircling wind descended smoothly to the ground, where it remained for only a moment before rising once again. For those few creatures who dared to look, they saw that where the seven men had once been standing, there now remained only the tools that they had dropped. As the wind continued to ascend, scattering leaves in every direction, the canopy yielded. Higher the wind travelled, and as the trees reverted in its wake, the fading blue mist became obscured from view. The last few leaves settled and the woodland once again fell silent.

- CHAPTER 18 -

Endless translucent streaks of light came to rest on the woodland floor, creating a shimmering patchwork of fallen leaves. The creatures of Speckled Wood stirred and emerged from hiding. Cold and confused, they gathered together and soon discussions of all kinds began to erupt. Some disbelieved what they had just witnessed, some argued over the reasons why it had happened and some were in total denial.

'You know not what you are saying!' Ruzig cried, disregarding the hasty comments of Yebbut the toad.

'It's outrageous!' Beamer screeched. 'Of course it really happened!'

'*Yebbut!* How is it possible for such a thing to happen? It defies all logic!'

'Logic?' Sirus overheard the discussion. 'Do you not know what caused the wind to act in such a way?'

'*Yebbut! Yebbut!* How can the spirits have been acting for good if they have taken Vulpash away?'

All those who heard his words fell silent. The fox's disappearance had been far from their thoughts. Turning away, they looked to the place where Vulpash had last been seen, their minds filled with regret. Maela was nearby, staring into the canopy, the words of her mother's song being solemnly offered up:

If only the trees could talk
I'd have much to say
About the way
I feel so alone on their canopy-moulting bay.

If only the trees could talk
I'd fill my day
In the daylight ray
Listening to tales of the old wood way.

If only the trees could talk
I would pray
On every day
For a special someone to come my way.

Balorn approached her. 'My Queen,' he spoke softly so as not to startle her. 'It is over. The war is won.'

'Is it?' Maela faced her companion. 'Look at this place, Balorn. It is destroyed. Never again will I wander freely and delight in the places that my mother used to love. Memories are all that I have left now. My peaceful haven destroyed. This is a grave day.'

Balorn looked upon his queen with deep concern. 'I know not what to say. But if there is anything that I can do ...'

'There is nothing that you can do. There is nothing

that anyone can do.' Maela looked with distant eyes over her homeland. 'But there may be something that I can do ...' She headed back to where the rest of the creatures were gathered, Balorn following close behind.

'Creatures of Speckled Wood,' Maela raised her voice, and at once all remaining discussions ceased. 'In many ways this is a great day. A day of victory. But let us not forget the strength and courage of our brave fellow companion, Vulpash. I have it on good authority that he will be looked after and we must all now rest our hope and trust with the spirits.' She paused, allowing time for the creatures to absorb her words.

A series of low mutterings broke out amongst the crowd, but only one voice dared to speak out. *'Yebbut!* Is he still alive?'

Maela raised a paw to call for silence. 'He is not dead. He will be returned to us just as he was.'

'Yebbut! How do you know this?'

The stillness in the crowd grew dark and ominous. How dare anyone ever question the sovereign's words?

'Your work here is done, my friends.' Maela was prepared to let the matter drop. 'It is time for you all to return to your homes and to rejoice in our victory.'

'*Yebbut!* How can we rejoice when one of our number is missing?' the toad persisted.

'My dear friend,' Maela looked down at him with woeful eyes. 'Have faith in what I tell you. I know you did not hear them, but the spirits of the trees do not lie, and neither do I. Go now, all of you, depart and return to your homes. You will be safe now. Balorn, Chief of the Council, will see to it that you all return safely.'

'My Queen?' Balorn questioned Maela as to her meaning.

'Dear Balorn,' she breathed. 'In you, I trust. Therefore, I need you to lead the creatures back to their homes and see that they are all safe.'

'But ...' Balorn hesitated. 'Forgive me, my Queen, but surely that is your duty, is it not?'

'Customarily, yes,' Maela replied with a glazed look.

'You mean to leave us, do you not?' Balorn's words seemed to go unnoticed. 'My Queen? Talk to me.'

At length, Maela's eyes refocused and she looked long at Balorn. His own eyes were urging her to speak. 'I will return,' she said at last. 'But you must understand, there are things that I need to do first – things that are important to me, and to me alone.'

After much thought, Balorn defiantly turned to address the waiting crowd. 'Friends,' he announced, 'our queen has commanded that we leave now. So come, dear friends, let us depart.' Without looking back, he dutifully joined the crowd as the creatures turned to leave. He shuffled his way towards the front, where he was met by Sirus and Famor.

Maela watched, joyous, yet disheartened, as the creatures of Speckled Wood departed. Soon she would be alone again, left only with her thoughts and memories for company. She did not linger to see the crowd leave, for she was desperate to survey her old homeland and, more importantly, to check on her hollow oak tree.

Her progress was slow, stopping at every tree stump she came to and every fallen branch, pausing each time in deep thought. She could not help but think back to how it had looked only a few days before.

'My Queen!'

Maela turned, startled. Balorn was approaching in haste.

'What is it?' Maela enquired as he came alongside. 'Why have you returned?'

'I could not let you do this on your own, my Queen, so I have come to offer you my assistance in any way that I can.'

'But what about the crowd? Did I not say that you were to see all the creatures safely returned home?'

'That you did. But I have taken it upon myself to pass that duty onto Sirus and Famor. They will not let me down, and they will not let you down, my Queen.'

Relief swept through Maela like a summer breeze. She had not wanted to be left on her own, but had not been able to find the words to ask Balorn to stay. 'It was ill fate that brought us together,' she said at last, 'and I feared that ill fate was near to tearing us apart.'

'You have no reason to fear, my Queen, for I will never leave you. I will remain your guide until my nights are no more.'

The two badgers exchanged fleeting glances before Maela began to walk again. Being so close to her hollow oak tree meant that, for now, she could think of nothing else, and soon she was clambering up the side of the leaf-covered mound that she knew so well. Apprehensively, she peered over the top and breathed a deep, weary sigh as Balorn came to her side. 'The most beautiful tree I have ever laid eyes upon,' she spoke in a dreamlike manner. 'That tree served me well.'

'That it did,' Balorn replied, noting the glazed look in Maela's eyes. 'But you have to let go now, my Queen. It is gone. No longer does your tree stand.'

As though emerging from a deep sleep, Maela blinked rapidly and shook her head. In her mind, she had just seen her tree exactly as she had left it, but the image that she had formed no longer existed. 'Just a stump,' she breathed, 'that is all. Just an empty stump.'

The ancient tree that had once stood so majestic and proud, now stood no taller than the height of a fox. Nearing it, Maela noticed some of her old bedding, scattered amongst the fallen leaves. The cavity that had once been her home was now desolate.

Maela placed an uneasy paw upon the stump, as though touching it would make her believe that what she was seeing was real. But she shook her head and immediately withdrew. 'This is all wrong. All wrong. This would never have happened if I had stayed here.'

'You cannot think like that, my Queen. This would have happened whether you were here or not. There is nothing you could have done to prevent it.'

'Nothing?' Maela exclaimed. 'Do you forget the power that I hold?'

'My Queen, I merely meant that –'

'I know what you meant, Balorn,' Maela's tone softened. 'And maybe you are right. This would have happened regardless, and it is clear to me now that there is nothing I can do.' She turned to face her companion. 'Forgive my harsh words.'

'It matters not,' Balorn replied, 'for I see how much this means to you.' Tears were forming in Maela's eyes. 'But weep not for your tree, my Queen.'

'I do not weep for my tree,' Maela breathed, trying to gather her thoughts. 'I weep ... for I now know where my heart lies.'

- CHAPTER 19 -

There lingered a sense of unease within the woodland as Maela led Balorn back towards the narrow stream. The sun was soon to be at its highest point, but clouds had formed, and the shadowless ground appeared grey and bleak. When they reached the stream's edge they stopped, and Maela drew in a long, deep breath, before releasing it as a sigh.

'What is it, my Queen?'

If ever there was a time when Maela needed strength, then it was now. 'I wanted to show you something,' she admitted with some hesitancy, 'but it no longer feels right to do so.'

Balorn gazed long at her, noticing the distant look in her eyes that had become so familiar. He waited, but said nothing; his silence urging her to continue.

Maela looked to the other side of the stream. 'That is where I used to dwell,' she said with affection. 'My mother's sett was beautiful. She kept it well. It was small, but we liked it. It was all that we had ever known. My home – the only place where I will ever feel I truly belonged. I remember my two brothers taking great delight in rolling around in their old bedding and kicking it at each other. My mother would never scold them. She allowed them their fun. She always appeared at ease with us, but I could tell, even from an early age, that something troubled her; something deep within her soul. My brothers never saw it and used to tease me whenever I mentioned it, but I know what I felt.'

'I never thought to ask you before,' Balorn began with remorse, 'but what were the names of your two brothers?'

'*Were?*' Maela exclaimed. 'You mean *are* – what *are* the names of my two brothers?'

Balorn held his tongue.

'They are named Mithlan and Braedor,' Maela spoke proudly, 'and I know that they are still alive. I am certain of that.'

'Braedor?' Balorn enquired.

'Yes. Why do you ask?'

'That was the name of your mother's predecessor: King Braedor of Speckled Wood. Your mother served him well. That is how he came to choose her as the next sovereign.'

His words sent a chill through Maela's spine, then a sudden cool breeze caused her to remember why she had led Balorn to the stream. 'Do you recall,' she said at length, 'when I told you about a secret place that my mother used to visit?'

'Indeed, I do.'

'It was just over there.' Maela directed Balorn's gaze upstream, to where an ancient alder tree stood; its twisted branches drooping. She then glanced down at the ring of alder cones on her foreleg. 'I wanted to tell Fira about it,' she went on. 'I wanted to bring him back here and show him. I held no trust in him the first time, and now I fear that time will not allow me to do so again.'

'But the war is ended, my Queen. This land will no longer be subject to man's destruction. You can continue to visit here as often as you wish.'

'That may be so. But what of Fira? What if he –?'

'He will pull through.' Balorn could see that this thought of Maela's had been troubling her for some time. 'There is no need for concern, I am sure.'

'But –'

'Maela, my Queen, concentrate on the matter at hand. Do not allow your mind to wander unnecessarily.'

The matter at hand was one that Maela was now determined to see through, and she nodded in agreement.

Walking at a steady pace, and allowing the cool breeze to ruffle her hair, she led Balorn upstream and stopped just short of where the alder tree stood. Looking up at its strange, twisted form, Balorn felt that in many ways it resembled one of the Coil Trees, yet he doubted whether any of its long, withered branches retained any form of life.

'This is it,' Maela whispered. 'Come and see.' She steered Balorn to the other side of the tree and told him to watch.

With great care, Maela positioned herself as close as

she dare to where the roots of the tree jutted and coiled out of the ground. She rested her paw gently upon one of the highest roots, which was smothered with patches of soft, green moss. The root began to quiver, and slowly it descended into the ground, exposing a dark, gaping chasm.

'So, here it is,' Maela took a step back. 'This is where I found the crown of leaves.'

'I – I have seen nothing of the like before,' Balorn's jaw trembled. 'I thought I knew everything about this woodland, but this, my Queen, this defies all belief.'

As though ignited by his words, the twisted root of the alder tree ascended and locked itself back into place. Then, as the cool breeze gathered in strength, a whispering voice issued from within the tree.

Maela, my Queen, have you returned to your tree?
Speak clearly, dear Maela, for I no longer see.

Balorn stared at Maela. 'So ... you already knew of the Coil Trees? You knew that their spirits could talk?'

'I did not,' Maela's eyes were fixed upon the tree. 'I – I had no idea. Many times I have visited here, yet this is the first time that I have heard it speak.'

'Then I think you had better answer it,' Balorn urged. The tree's branches twitched as though agitated.

A thought then occurred to Maela. How was it that Balorn could hear the voice? Curiously, she edged closer to the tree. 'I am Maela,' she announced, 'Queen of Speckled Wood.'

The voice within the tree responded at once.

Though I cannot see, my hearing is fair,
And you are not Maela who left me her share.

Her share? Maela frowned, wondering at these words. Her expression then brightened. 'The crown!' she declared. 'Of course! You speak of my mother's crown. But I am Queen Maela now. I wear the crown. Do you not remember me taking it only a few days ago?'

Forgive me, dear Maela, for I should have seen
That you would be next in line for the queen.

Of course I remember you taking the crown,
For I would not let any other go down.

But Maela, your mother entrusted to me
Far more than her crown, as you will now see.

The ground beneath the badgers' paws began to tremble as the twisted roots of the tree contracted, its branches swaying violently in the strengthening breeze.

Standing firm, Maela gave Balorn an awkward yet quizzical glance. He appeared as though he was ready to fight should the need arise.

The trembling ceased and, as the cool breeze settled, the mossy root began to descend on its own. But this time, instead of revealing an empty chasm, a small brown object appeared, hovering in the centre. No longer was the hole dark and foreboding. It glowed now, with a white, iridescent light.

Maela felt strangely drawn to the object, staring at it fixedly. Her mother's scent was rife, giving her an overwhelming desire to take hold of it.

'Be careful, my Queen,' Balorn warned as Maela extended her paw.

The object was prickly and slightly warm to the touch. Maela held it with extreme care, examining it closely as she withdrew from the tree. It was a tightly closed beech nut, no bigger than the pad on her paw.

Queen Maela, your mother, she left that for you
And gave me instruction for what you should do:

Maela listened to the words, staring intently at the nut.

This day you should rest. Take sleep where you can,
Allowing your dreams to be distant from man.

There you will witness what lies in the past.
But do not there linger for it will not last.

The spirit of the alder tree did not speak again. The root ascended back into place, the branches yielded and withered once more, and the last trace of the breeze faded away.

'Well,' Maela said at last, turning to Balorn, 'what do you make of that?'

- CHAPTER 20 -

Balorn looked long overhead. Dark clouds were forming. The departure of the cool breeze had left him with a sense of foreboding that was not easy to shake off. 'We should seek rest,' he said at length, as though disturbed by his own thoughts. 'Come, my Queen.'

He started to walk downstream, but Maela felt reluctant to leave the familiar surroundings. Looking around at what was left, she remembered how it used to be. The swathes of bluebells that her two brothers used to chase her through. Her beloved trees flourishing in the summer sun. The perfect hiding place in her hollow oak tree where her brothers never found her. She had known every single tree as though it were a part of her, able to run between their trunks with eyes closed, knowing each one's location. Alder, birch, beech and oak, all gone now. All gone. Her memory faded until all she could see was the devastation once more.

And now she was torn. Torn between returning with Balorn, back to the East, and continuing with her duties as Queen of Speckled Wood, or staying in the West, dwelling on the past and clinging on to the hope that one day her brothers would return there.

With her anguish too great to bear, she closed her eyes and remembered again what she would be turning her back on. She then looked ahead and noticed that Balorn had stopped. He was facing her, his solemn eyes pleading with her to join him.

Still undecided, Maela glanced down at the beech nut, still in her paw. *You will not fail.* Her mother's words returned to her and at last she knew what she must do.

Carefully pushing the nut into the ring of alder cones around her foreleg, she took a long, deep breath, telling herself that this is what her mother would want. Then, after taking one lasting glance back over her shoulder to where the ancient alder tree stood, she realigned the crown on her head and began on her way.

The two badgers walked in silence. Balorn could not bring himself to approach the subject of the beech nut for fear of burdening Maela further. Maela, however, could think of nothing else. Her mind was brimming with endless possibilities about the significance of the nut. What would it reveal? Would it do something on its own or would she have to do something to it? It was not long before her thoughts turned again to her mother. She felt an overwhelming sense that she was still with her, watching over her, providing for her in her time of need. It was enough for Maela to know that the nut would aid her in some way, and with this knowledge she began to feel lightheaded.

They had not walked far when Balorn decided that

they should stop. He had noticed how frail Maela had become and was soon scraping together a pile of dry leaves, dragging them towards a thicket of bramble. 'This will do for now,' he said.

Despite her frailty, Maela dutifully helped Balorn arrange the bedding and soon they were settled, side by side, concealed and sheltered beneath the thicket.

Dark shadows passed over the two badgers as they drifted unhindered into their separate dreams. The woodland around them stood still, as though waiting, watching for something to happen.

Before long, Balorn was awoken by an ominous feeling. Raising his nose high into the air, he sniffed hard, then sat up and looked around. Beside him, lay the tightly curled figure of Maela, her crown at her side, and his expression softened with relief as he watched her sleep. The beech nut was tucked between her head and her paws, but no longer was it closed. Taking a closer look, Balorn witnessed the nut opening. It began to glow with an orange, shimmering light, as though a raging fire was burning from deep within.

Maela slept on, unaware of what was happening right under her nose, listening intently to her mother's soft voice ...

*

The light of day faded as Balorn continued to watch over his Queen. Every now and again her paws twitched, as though she was locked in some kind of harrowing brawl with no way of escape. But Balorn resisted the urge to wake her. He kept a wary eye on the beech nut and saw at length that the orange glow was waning.

Maela's eyes flickered and she released a heavy sigh.

'My Queen?' Balorn whispered.

A gentle tap on her paw caused Maela to start. Eyes wide, she stared into the semidarkness. 'Father?' she called. 'Where are you? Do not leave me again!'

'My Queen,' Balorn repeated. 'It is I, Balorn. You were having a dream – that is all. Just a dream.'

Maela's eyes slipped into focus and rested upon her companion. 'Balorn,' she uttered, 'that was no dream.' She paused to collect her thoughts. 'I have just witnessed something from my past – or rather, from my mother's past. And this –' she gazed down at the beech nut, appearing not to notice that it was now open, '– this held the power to show me.' She held the nut aloft and stared at it in wonder.

'What did you see?'

Moved by Balorn's voice, Maela glanced at him briefly, offering him a weak smile, before gazing high into the canopy. 'We should go,' she said. 'It is time for me to leave here. Too long have I already lingered.'

This was not the answer that Balorn had expected, but he was pleased nonetheless that Maela felt able at last to leave her homeland in a positive frame of mind. But Maela did not just feel positive. She felt stronger; stronger than she had ever felt before, for now she knew the answers to many of the questions that had been troubling her for far too long.

Before continuing with their journey, the two badgers agreed that there was one last thing that needed to be done. They returned, therefore, to the place where the men had last been seen. Their discarded tools remained scattered on the ground and the few traces of russet-red fur served as cruel reminders of Vulpash's disappearance.

Balorn scratched purposefully at the fallen leaves and, before long, both he and Maela were digging down into the soil. They worked in silence until they had before them a deep, narrow pit. One by one, they then dragged the tools into the pit, relishing in the clank of metal against metal as spade fell upon axe and saw fell upon spade.

Once all of the tools had been buried, and Balorn had scattered the remainder of the soil, the companions looked upon their work with a sense of pride and satisfaction.

'Now, I can leave,' Maela declared. 'The past is put to rest and I can leave.'

- CHAPTER 21 -

Meandering through the trees, the two badgers kept their pace steady, each with their own mind occupied with recent events, each longing for the other to speak. Maela carried the open beech nut within the ring of alder cones as before, and every so often she glanced at it, allowing the memories of her mother's past to return. She knew that Balorn was eager to learn of what she knew, but there was one other with whom she wanted to discuss the matter first, so for now, she decided, Balorn would have to wait.

Darkness surrounded them as they crossed the narrow stream, and whilst Maela continued to fathom the workings of the small wooden bridge, they continued their journey along the Queen's Path. Treading carefully over the stony ground, the clearing soon came into view, and it was there that Maela and Balorn took time to rest and find food. Maela thought back to the first time that she had been there, and a chill cut through her at the memory of having lost her mother's crown. A swift readjustment of the crown now made her feel far more at ease.

A gentle breeze swept through the clearing, bringing with it the unmistakeable scent of Balorn's territory.

'It feels good, does it not?' Maela remarked, sensing Balorn's delight at returning to his homeland.

'That it does,' he replied. 'And yet, I cannot help but think that our return will be marred with feelings of unrest.'

As they set off for the last part of their journey, Balorn continued to fear the reaction of their homecoming. Maela, meanwhile, kept her mind occupied on the words of her mother's songs, trying to distance herself from the emotions that were spiralling within her, knowing that she would soon have to face up to the reality of what happened to her mother.

A short distance on, Maela came to an abrupt halt.

'What is it, my Queen?'

'Earlan!' Maela exclaimed. 'Can you not hear him? The blackbird sings his song!' Balorn stopped to listen. 'We are being welcomed back, Balorn! We are being welcomed!'

For far too long, Maela had dreamt of following the sweet voice of the blackbird, believing that it was calling her to a better place, and now, at last, she was living her dream.

With their spirits lifted, the two badgers picked up their pace and followed Earlan's voice. Soon, birds of all kinds were joining in with the joyous tunes, and cries of elation swept through the trees. Sirus and Beamer were the first to greet them.

'Welcome home! Welcome home!' Sirus flicked his

tail with glee, bowing graciously in front of his queen.

'I am glad to see you both safe and unharmed,' Beamer said. He too gave a bow and presented Maela with a garland of ivy.

Maela removed her crown to accept her gift and soon found herself lost amid a crowd of creatures, all welcoming her and congratulating her on leading them successfully into battle. Balorn was overcome by the reaction, and he looked upon his queen with pride as she replaced her crown, feeling certain that fate had played a major role in bringing her to power and to saving Speckled Wood from man's destruction.

The creatures then proceeded to chant:

The war is won! The war is won!
Queen Maela is seated
And man is defeated!
The war is won! The war is won!

It was easy for Maela to forget that there were far more pressing matters that needed her attention. She was completely absorbed, having never experienced such a celebration before. But as she looked into the crowd, casting her eyes over the array of creatures amassed before her, not a single fox could she see. She turned at once to Balorn and expressed her concerns.

'Yes,' he nodded. 'It is as I feared. Come, my Queen, we must find my sisters.'

Pulling away from the bustling crowd, the two badgers hastened in the direction of Balorn's sett. But whilst Balorn feared the worst, Maela felt comforted by the festivities that were continuing behind them, feeling that if something was amiss, then the atmosphere would be vastly different.

Despite holding on to this positive thought, when they reached the entrance to Balorn's sett, the air that greeted them was anything but welcoming. Balorn sniffed hard at the cool night air. A pile of discarded bedding nearby caught his attention, and without hesitation he scampered into the tunnel. Maela hurried after him, and moments later, she was peering over his shoulder into the chamber where they had last seen Fira. Vacant, apart from one or two dry leaves, the chamber was unusually cold.

'What does this mean?' Maela asked, uncertain that she wanted to know the answer.

'I fear,' Balorn choked, 'that it can mean only one thing.'

He hurriedly left the sett, Maela following close behind. The air outside was no more welcoming than it had been before, and as the celebrations continued in the distance, they desperately scanned the area for other signs of life. Balorn then spotted his two sisters running towards him.

'Our brother has returned!' Belana exclaimed.

'Oh, dearest brother!' Baralda cried.

The two sisters came to a halt and bowed before their queen.

'Where is Fira?' Balorn demanded to know. 'And Famor? I do not see them here!'

A look of remorse entered Belana's eyes. 'How I have feared this moment,' she said, more to herself. 'Oh, Balorn, you must forgive us.'

'Just tell me where they are!' Balorn insisted.

'I feared that you would react so,' Belana said. 'I told them this, and yet –' she glanced solemnly between her brother and her queen. 'Come. Let us delay no longer.'

The two sisters led Balorn and Maela towards the council meeting place.

'Why are we going this way?' Balorn enquired.

'All will be revealed,' Belana told him.

The moon was high above them by the time the badgers reached the ring of hazel trees. Before them stood the figures of two foxes.

Maela hurried forward, eager to lay eyes on Fira and to learn that he was well. But she had taken no more than a few steps into the ring when she stopped in her tracks. The fox closest to her was Famor, who stood there echoing her gaze; eyes wide, full of remorse. The other fox, much older in years, was not at all the companion that Maela had hoped to see there.

Balorn, breaking away from his sisters, hurried to Maela's side. 'Vulpash,' he said with exasperation. 'I might have known you would be behind all this secrecy. How long have you been back?'

'Never mind that now,' Maela cut in. 'Tell me, where is Fira?'

'I am here.'

- CHAPTER 22 -

Maela spun round. Standing tall in front of one of the slender hazel trees was Fira; his coat shimmering as though flecks of moonlight were dancing around him, his amber eyes sparkling above a knowing smile.

The fox approached his queen and bowed low.

Belana, Baralda and Famor gathered around, looking upon Maela with sympathetic eyes, whilst Balorn, sharing the feelings of his queen, could not help but stare at Fira.

Feeling as though the whole woodland was watching her, waiting for her silence to be broken, Maela at last felt compelled to speak. 'My dear Fira,' she uttered. 'I cannot tell you how good it is to see you again.'

'Nor I you,' Fira replied.

The two companions were captivated in each other's presence, so much so that they failed to notice Vulpash slinking towards them.

Ahem.

Maela turned and glared disapprovingly, rebuking Vulpash for his distraction.

'Forgive me, Queen Maela, but I must speak with

you alone.'

'Not now. It will have to wait.'

'But it is of the highest importance. There are matters we need to discuss, and I –'

'No!' Maela cut in. 'This is not the time.'

'But if I could just –'

The sound of faint voices and scampering feet distracted the group's attention.

'Of course they will want to join us,' one of the voices said. 'Why would they not?'

'They may have other things to do,' the second voice replied. 'More important things to do with their time.'

'But this *is* their time ... You mark my words, they will want to –'

Two figures emerged, bumbling through the ring of trees. They stopped in their tracks, tripping over one another's feet, and landed face down amongst the leaves. Sirus and One-Eyed Mas then raised their heads ashamedly.

'– join us,' One-Eyed Mas finished his sentence.

'Join you?' Balorn frowned upon the two friends. 'Join you where?'

'At the celebration of course!'

Sirus jabbed One-Eyed Mas in his side.

'Ow! What did you –?' Guided by Sirus's expression, One-Eyed Mas realised the error of his ways and spoke no more.

Balorn turned to Fira. 'This celebration is yours as much as it is all of ours,' he said. Then turning to Maela he added, 'We should all go.'

'But –' Vulpash flicked his tail indignantly, 'I have not yet spoken!'

Maela looked beyond the darkened trees. 'The air is clear. All that had to be said this night has already been said. We have no further business here.'

'But –'

'Did you not hear me, Vulpash? I said, the air is clear.' Maela looked long at the fox until a hint of recognition in her eyes finally told him her meaning.

*

With Sirus and One-Eyed Mas taking the lead, the companions made their way back to the celebration. Filled with immense sorrow, Maela cast her eyes over Fira's wounded shoulder. 'Forgive me,' she said, 'but I did not get the chance to ask how you are.'

'Apart from my shoulder, my wounds were not deep. I have been well cared for.' Fira glanced ahead towards Belana and Baralda. 'The only thing that pains me now is that I could not join you in your battle against man. Famor relayed to me all that happened and I sorely regret not being a part of it.'

'It matters not.'

'It does to me. If I had only stood up to Vulpash sooner, then –'

Maela shuddered as a series of painful flashbacks speared her mind. She took a deep breath to steady herself and wondered what Vulpash was so eager to talk to her about. Was it anything to do with her mother's past?

'Maela?' Balorn's voice caused Maela to start. 'What is it, my Queen?'

Maela wished with every part of her soul that she could tell Balorn what she knew, but she could not.

'The past is put to rest,' Balorn continued, '– that is what you told me. So we must now look to the future.'

'But ... it is not,' Maela hesitated, '– not until I have spoken with Vulpash.'

Balorn and Fira looked to each other for enlightenment, but none was found.

'Very well,' Balorn said at last. 'Until then, let us enjoy the celebration and see to it that our minds are rested.'

On their arrival, spirits were lifted, and the creatures of Speckled Wood cheered and welcomed the companions. The air was filled with mirth, and rows upon rows of songbirds lined the branches of the trees, singing in perfect harmony. Maela gazed at them in wonder. Earlan then flew down and landed just in front of her. In his beak, he held a sprig of plump blackberries, which he graciously dropped at Maela's feet.

'A gift for our queen,' he chirruped.

'Thank you.' Maela stooped to savour the sweet scent of the berries. 'You are most kind.'

As Earlan flew back up to continue singing in the trees, Balorn and Fira watched Maela eating the berries. It was the first time they had seen her looking relaxed.

'Do you know why Vulpash was so insistent to speak with Maela?' Balorn whispered.

Fira shook his head. 'Whatever it is, no good will come of it, I am sure.'

- CHAPTER 23 -

Maela took her leave and sat beside a thicket of bramble, her crown and garland at her side, her head held low. Close by, the creatures of Speckled Wood continued to rejoice, but Maela sought solitude from what had been an exhausting few nights. Daylight would soon be upon her and she felt this was her last opportunity to consider what she was going to say to Vulpash. Closing her eyes, she drew in a deep, cooling breath.

Snap!

The all too familiar sound turned Maela's stomach. Through wide eyes, she stared blindly ahead of her.

'I hope I did not disturb you,' came a voice from the shadows.

The dark figure of Vulpash approached. 'What do you want?' Maela raised herself up.

'I mean you no harm. I simply wondered if we could talk now.'

Maela wished that she had had more time to herself, to prepare her thoughts and to reflect more upon what the beech nut had enabled her to see. But she could delay the inevitable no longer. 'Very well,' she agreed. 'I will listen to what you have to say.'

'I have wronged you, my Queen,' Vulpash lowered his eyes in shame. 'Or rather, I wronged your mother. And I now ask for your forgiveness.'

'*Forgiveness?*' Maela choked. 'And what exactly am I supposed to be forgiving you for?'

Vulpash pawed at the ground before him. 'It is all my fault,' he admitted. 'It cannot be denied that I have done many wrongs in my life, but there is one thing that is now burdening me with such force that I can bear it no longer.'

Maela held silent, eager to hear a confession.

'I have never withheld my desire to become ruler of Speckled Wood,' Vulpash continued, 'so much so that on more than one occasion it has driven me to carry out the lowest acts of deceit and disloyalty to my companions.' He paused momentarily to gather his thoughts. 'However,' he went on, directing his gaze at Maela, 'there is one act of mine that you should now be made aware of.'

A profound look of fear was evident behind the fox's eyes. 'And what is that?' Maela asked, uncertain as to whether she wanted to know.

'I did a foolish thing. I caused your mother to leave. I lied to her. I deceived her. It is all my fault. I did not mean for it to be like this. It is all my –'

'What did you do?' Maela cut in.

'She left because of me. I told her many lies, not least that if she remained here as Queen, then she would bring disrepute to the name of Speckled Wood.'

Maela struggled with the thoughts in her mind, uncertain how to proceed. 'But, why?' she asked. 'Why would you do such a thing?'

'I was desperate,' Vulpash explained. 'I wanted so much to become ruler that I told her that all the other creatures were talking about her behind her back; that they had lost their confidence in her and were holding secret talks, discussing how best to get her to step down. As a result, I advised her to leave without a word and to stay away until the tension had died down.'

Maela shook her head. 'She would never have listened to you. Why would she?'

'Because I knew what she had done,' Vulpash lowered his eyes. 'She was in no condition to continue. Nobody else knew of this, and so I thought it would be to her advantage to have her cubs away from here and to return the following summer.'

An uncomfortable picture was beginning to form in Maela's mind of the events leading up to her birth. But why was it that only Vulpash knew of her mother's condition? And why had none of the other creatures ever said anything more about her mother's sudden disappearance? Curiously, she questioned the fox further.

'It remains so that none of the other creatures know the circumstances of your mother's disappearance. I knew only because ...' Vulpash swallowed hard.

'Go on,' Maela urged.

'Because I saw her at her lowest point and she

confided in me. She had recently met with another of her kind, from the neighbouring woodland, and he was more than willing to console your mother during her state of distress.'

'The distress that you had caused.'

'Yes. Indeed. But –' Vulpash turned away from Maela's accusing eyes.

'What happened after that?' Maela pressed on.

Vulpash thought carefully before answering. 'You must understand that your mother was not herself, so I simply suggested that she take some time alone to think over what had happened. She left soon after and was never seen here again.'

Maela glanced down at the crown, then closed her eyes, taking a few mind-numbing moments to allow the fox's words to sink in. Somewhere in her consciousness, she was mildly aware of the continued laughter and singing at the celebration, and wished that she had remained there.

When at last she found herself thinking clearly again, she replaced the crown upon her head and raised her chin. 'Why now? Why are you telling me this now?'

A pained expression contorted Vulpash's face. 'I saw the light,' he said. 'I looked into the light of the tree spirits as they were taking me away. The words they spoke to me ... I will never forget such pain.'

'Pain?' Maela frowned. 'They inflicted pain upon you?'

'I speak not of physical pain, but of the painful truth that was told to me. I was made to realise the error of my ways and to seek forgiveness from the one who I wronged.'

'And you took that to mean me?'

'Of course,' Vulpash shrugged. 'Who else could it mean?'

'My mother?'

'But – your mother is no longer here. If she were, then I would surely have sought forgiveness from her.'

'That may be so, but the fact remains that you are only asking for forgiveness because the tree spirits told you to. Is that not so?'

'Yes, that is so.'

'Then why should I believe that you are sincere? If you had spoken of this sooner, then I would have thought differently of you; seen you in a different light, but you have not changed. Is it not so that you now fear my reaction?'

'Fear?' Vulpash shook his head. 'No. I feel no fear.'

'Then maybe you should.' Maela stood up and started to walk away.

'But I tell you the truth!' Vulpash implored. 'Why would I lie about this?'

'That is what we would all like to know.'

Maela stopped in her tracks as the figures of Balorn and Fira emerged from behind a nearby oak tree.

'Well?' Balorn continued, staring at Vulpash. 'We are waiting.'

For a moment, Vulpash resembled his old self again. Consumed with rage, his dark eyes flickered wildly between Balorn and Fira, but he knew that it was not worth the fight. With a sharp intake of breath, he hung his head in shame. 'It is the truth,' he muttered. 'It is the truth.'

Maela and Balorn exchanged glances, neither of them knowing what to say.

Fira then took it upon himself to speak. 'I, for one, am not prepared to believe what you say, Vulpash. I knew Maela's mother well and I know she held trust in me.' Vulpash looked up, but did not speak. 'She had many friends here, and I fail to believe that she would have left because of some misadventure.'

'I know what you think of me, Firana, and you have every reason not to believe me, but you must understand that I was desperate. I needed her out of the way. I so wanted to be ruler of Speckled Wood ... Many times I tried to persuade her that things were not as they seemed, but she would not listen. In the end, I took drastic action and she knew then that she could not remain here and have everyone talking about her.'

Still finding this hard to believe, Fira exclaimed, 'If all that you say is true, then why are you telling us now?'

Having already heard the reason behind Vulpash's sudden change of heart, Maela offered up a silent prayer to her mother. She was desperate to hear her voice again; in desperate need of her guidance as she could not foresee an end to the situation before her.

A sudden cold breeze ruffled the hair on Maela's back. She became engulfed in darkness, her world fading away as the strengthening wind encircled her.

The spirits of the trees were with her once more.

Maela, our Queen, we respond to your word.
We know how you feel about what you've just heard.

Dear Maela, your courage and strength have shone through,
But we know of the fears that lie hidden in you.

'Fears?' Maela's tenacious cry echoed through the wind. 'What do you know of my fears?'

There is no need to fight this alone. We beseech,
Think back to what lay in the fruit of the beech.

Maela looked down at her foreleg, her eyes resting upon the open beech nut. 'I have not forgotten what I saw. I just do not know what I am to do.'

We, as the spirits, can only advise:
First you must search for the truth among lies.

Do not take to heart all that was said,
Through no fault of your own you have been misled.

Your mother's encounter was not as it seems,
But was one of the fox's more devilish schemes.

Maela frowned. 'I do not understand. Are you saying that – that Vulpash knew what would happen to my mother when she met with this other badger?'

The truth is now known; there's no more to be told,
So take heed, Queen Maela – his fate you now hold!

Swirling clouds of grey and white mist loomed above Maela's head. The darkness was broken, but she could not bear to look. Squeezing her eyes tightly shut, she cried, 'Wait! Please, wait! I still do not know what to do!'

Whatever you decide, whatever you do,
Be guided by what you know to be true.

Have faith in your feelings and trust in your soul,
For you are the ruler – that is your role.

- CHAPTER 24 -

The voice of the spirits faded, and so too did the swirling mist. No longer in darkness, Maela's world was once again in the moonlit woodland and she sensed that her fellow companions were close. When at last she felt able to open her eyes, she found Fira still trying to entice the truth out of Vulpash. 'Is it not so,' he was saying, 'that you are now trying to use the same lies and deceit to persuade our present Queen Maela to stand down – just as you did with her mother?'

'Not so!' Vulpash exclaimed.

'Can you not admit that you are lying?' Fira persisted. 'Have you told so many lies in your life that you no longer know what the truth is?'

'It *is* the truth! I tell not a word of a lie!'

'*Enough!*' Maela's voice echoed with authority. As her fellow companions turned to face her, she readjusted her crown and stood tall. 'I have heard enough. This ends now.'

'You are right, my Queen,' Balorn bowed graciously. 'As soon as Vulpash has apologised for telling so many lies –'

'No,' Maela stepped in, 'for he has no need to apologise.'

'But, my Queen –'

'I said no, Balorn, for Vulpash speaks the truth.'

Maela's words resounded through the trees. Balorn and Fira stared at their Queen with disbelieving eyes, and Vulpash, full of bewilderment, wondered if he should fear her reaction after all.

'Before any of you start to think that I have lost my mind,' Maela continued, 'you should know that the events leading up to my mother's disappearance were known to me before now.'

Vulpash's tail twitched.

'However,' Maela added, 'there is just one thing that still bothers me ... and that is how you, Vulpash, came to be so involved.'

'I told you,' Vulpash fixed his eyes upon Maela. 'I saw your mother not long after her meeting with –'

'Ah, yes,' Maela cut in, 'her meeting. Tell me again how she came to meet with Baddrae.'

Vulpash's eyes flickered from side to side. 'How do you know his –?' he began to ask before thinking better of it. 'I am not sure. She must have just wandered off and –'

'And just happened to meet another badger, who just happened to be there when she needed company? I think not.' Maela watched Vulpash attentively. 'Now, here is what I think happened. I think that you arranged for Baddrae to meet with my mother for one reason only.'

'Now look,' Vulpash raised himself up. 'I thought you said that you believed all that I told you.'

'Oh yes, I do. Or at least I believe the rest of what told me, for I already know it to be true. But telling the truth does not come easy to you, does it? Your tongue was always going to trip you up.'

'My Queen,' Fira interjected. 'Pardon my asking, but *how* do you know this to be true?'

'Ah, dear Fira,' Maela's eyes softened. 'How do you think it is that I came to learn so much about your kind? You say that you knew my mother well, so you doubtless know that she would have found a way of letting me know what really happened to her.'

Without further exchange, her words satisfied Fira's curiosity and it was then that Vulpash knew he was beaten.

'So what happens now?' he asked gingerly. 'What are you going to do?'

Maela released a heavy sigh, looking long into the distance. 'It seems as though I need to make a decision – a decision as to whether I should banish you from this part of the woodland or whether I should banish you from Speckled Wood altogether.'

Vulpash opened his mouth to protest, but the words would not come. He had not expected Maela's reaction to be so harsh. He had thought, or rather hoped, that at the very least she would have allowed things to continue as they were, particularly as he had taken it upon himself to broach the subject of her mother in the first place.

Balorn and Fira stood silent, waiting in anticipation to hear what Maela would decide. They too had not expected her words to be so harsh.

But how could anyone truly know how Maela was feeling? For far too long she had lived without the knowledge of her mother's past, and learning of the anguish that she had been forced to endure was too much for her to bear. And there she was now, standing face to face with the one who had caused the distress, holding his fate in her paws. She had no choice but to banish him, one way or the other, but knew that whatever she decided was going to affect the future of the woodland. Did she really want all the other creatures to find out what happened to their previous queen? And did she want to live with the constant questions as to why Vulpash no longer lived there? In confused desperation, she recalled the words of the spirits:

Whatever you decide, whatever you do,
Be guided by what you know to be true.

Have faith in your feelings and trust in your soul,
For you are the ruler – that is your role.

Adjusting her crown, Maela could ignore the anxious eyes of her companions no longer. And so, after much thought, and much searching of her soul, she finally announced, 'The decision is made!'

*

The first streaks of daylight flickered through the trees as Maela and Balorn sat together beside the entrance to his sett. 'I can only imagine how you must be feeling.'

Balorn was concerned that since announcing her decision, Maela had not spoken a word to anyone. 'But you did right, my Queen. Do not allow yourself to think otherwise.'

At hearing his words, Maela looked up. 'I did not do it for his sake. I did it purely for my own selfish reasons. If he had not arranged for my mother to meet with Baddrae, then I would not be here. So you see, dear Balorn, in my eyes he did no wrong.'

'As I said, my Queen – you did right.'

'But did I? You may think so, and many of the other creatures may think so too, and I dare say that I will be looked upon far more highly now, but what of my mother? Have you not stopped to consider the suffering that she must have gone through, knowing that she could never return here and continue her sovereignty as before? She gave up everything because of what he did and, more importantly, she gave up everything for me and my two brothers.' As she spoke, Maela caught a glimmer of remorse in Balorn's eyes. 'So now can you imagine how I am feeling?'

Balorn so desperately wanted to say the right thing, but was unsure of how to react. He therefore pondered deeply before replying. 'You must be wondering about your father.'

This was the last thing that Maela had expected him to say. 'My father?' she spoke in a dreamlike manner. 'Yes, I suppose I am. Or at least I have been. But I am not ready to go searching for him yet. Time will tell as to whether I will ever come to need him. Besides, he may not want to know me. He may not even be alive.' She paused for a moment, her brow furrowed. 'No,' she went on, 'I have much to do here. I am happy here, and I am happy being here with you.' Her face softened as she gazed at her companion.

'I will always be here for you,' Balorn echoed the tone of Maela's voice, 'and I will be your guide for as long as you need me.'

'Then I will be safe in that knowledge.'

As the sun started to rise, filling the woodland with fresh hope, the two badgers were last seen entering Balorn's sett. A short distance away, deep within the shadows, a knowing smile rested easily beneath a russet red snout, and with a flick of a tail, it was gone.

ABOUT THE AUTHOR

S.W. Teal gets most of her inspiration from nature and can often be found walking through woodlands and parks with her notebook and camera.

The original idea for *The Queen of Speckled Wood* developed whilst she was working as a volunteer Wildlife Care Assistant for the RSPCA, which is where much of her research into the characters took place.

It is fair to say that S.W. Teal loves the natural world, but she also has a fascination for the supernatural, which is evident in many of the stories she writes.

ACKNOWLEDGMENTS

I would firstly like to thank my family and friends, who have supported and encouraged me throughout this creative process.

Special thanks goes to Kelly Whitaker-Hughes for writing the words to *'If Only the Trees Could Talk'*. Without it, Maela may not have had such a beautiful song to sing.

Thanks also to George for patiently believing in me and for saying that this should be made into a film.

And to those who read the story first, thank you for steering me in the right direction.

Finally, thanks must go to the wonderful people who work tirelessly to protect Speckled Wood and its inhabitants. Yes, Speckled Wood actually exists, almost exactly as I describe it, and so thanks must go to those who make the woodland accessible for all to enjoy.

Discover more on my Facebook page @swteal

Printed in Great Britain
by Amazon